WINDBREAK
GRYPHON RIDERS BOOK THREE

Windbreak:
Gryphon Riders Trilogy Book Three

DEREK ALAN SIDDOWAY

Chapter 1

"Talus," Seppo said again. "My name is Talus."

No one in the war council spoke. Eva stared, open-mouthed as Seppo reached out and lifted the Wonder in his hand. It was a spherical ball of unknown black metal — her father had stolen it from the ruins of Palantis in the far east. He'd sacrificed his life so that she and her friends could bring it back to Rhylance. They hoped it was the key to defeating the Smelterborn: enchanted, armored golems twice the size of a man that were nigh impossible to kill. Forged to spread death, chaos, and destruction, the Smelterborn knew no emotion and felt no pain.

The guards stirred. Hands went for swords. Seppo looked up from the Wonder, his round, metal, helmeted head swiveling in confusion, the two blue orbs that made up the golem's eyes questioning the reactions of the humans around him.

"Don't hurt him!"

Eva jumped out of her seat and ran to Seppo's side. The Scrawls, masters of runes and lore who had been studying the Wonder and presenting their findings to the council, all took a step back when Eva neared the golem. The last thing Eva had to tell anyone was not to hurt the golem. Seppo stood at least a head over the tallest of men. His body, comprised of iron plates, gave him the appearance of a giant, walking, talking suit of armor, empty save for whatever magic gave him life.

Soot, her foster-father and Seppo's owner, joined Eva and Seppo. He placed a cautious hand on Eva to back her away and stared at his ironclad friend with suspicion.

"What d'you mean your name is Talus?" Soot asked the golem. "We've been together twenty years and you've never said that name before."

Seppo pointed a shaky iron finger as thick as Eva's wrist at the dark Wonder. "It made me...remember things. Things from my past but they're still shrouded. Talus was my name once. I'm sure of it."

Eva was surprised to hear confusion and a trace of fear in Seppo's clipped metallic voice. She'd only heard fragments of the story of how Soot came to own the golem. The smith had been part of a journey to the eastern part of Altaris. The expedition included Aleron — Eva's father — her uncle Andor and several others. They'd eventually found their way to Palantis, the island home of the Ancients who'd disappeared centuries before.

The expedition explored the city ruins, unearthing a random assortment of artifacts including Seppo, a rune-engraved sword Eva's father had given her before he died and a necklace he'd brought back for her mother, among others. Throughout history, many people had found other relics of the Ancients, deemed "Wonders" for their miraculous and improbable magical powers. However improbable it seemed, Seppo spoke as if he had lived in such a bygone era.

"What do you remember?" Soot asked in a sharp voice.

Seppo lifted up a gauntleted metal hand to rub the back of his head, like a gigantic old man lost in thought. "I... It's all a whirl of places and faces. Something terrible happened and I was there, but beyond that, I do not know."

"So we're no closer to defeating the Smelterborn than we were before," King Adelar, Eva's other uncle, said.

"The First Forge!" Seppo's panicked voice rang throughout the hall. "That was what I went back for. The First Forge must be destroyed!"

The king looked at Andor, the Lord Commander of the

Windsworn. "What is this First Forge? Did you come across it in your explorations?"

The lord commander pursed his lips and thought for a long moment before shaking his head. "Who knows? Everything was in ruin and rubble, grown over by grass and weeds. I'll look through my journals and the maps we drew of Palantis but, without knowing what I'm looking for, I doubt it'll do much good. There certainly wasn't anything spewing out Smelterborn when we were there, I can tell you that."

"How do we know this... this thing can be trusted?" One of the nobles asked, pointing at Seppo. "All I see is yet another golem. Maybe it has been passing them information all these years!"

Several others shouted in agreement. Seppo spun around, mouth plate opening in shock.

"Stop it!" Eva shouted, cutting through the angry crowd. "You're scaring him! I grew up with Seppo — he wouldn't hurt a fly. Leave him alone."

Although her heart pounded to be the center of attention in the court, Eva's anger carried her past her timidity.

"Out of everyone here, I'm one of the few who've even seen a Smelterborn," she said. "Seppo is not like them and I can prove it!"

Eva reached for the gold chain around her neck and withdrew the stone from beneath her shirt. She thrust her mother's Wonder up toward Seppo's face. The rose, gold and blue-colored lights danced off his muted gray armor. Otherwise, nothing happened.

"The Smelterborn can't stand the light from the stone," Eva explained. "If Seppo were the same as them, he would be on his knees right now."

The magical stone on Eva's necklace had helped her defeat several Smelterborn in the past but in their recent journey, she and her friends learned there were hundreds — maybe thousands — of the golems.

A few nobles returned to their chairs, but Eva saw their suspicious eyes linger on the golem. Tempers and voices raised until the entire council's order collapsed in a cacophony of shouts and hand waving — complete madness.

At last, the king rose and restored order with a few shouts and hard, steely-eyed glares at some of the more outspoken attendees. When the room fell silent, he sat back down. Eva looked at her two uncles and saw the pronounced lines of worry and exhaustion on their faces, marks of running a kingdom and a military order for decades.

"Until we learn more about this First Forge and what connection Seppo has to it, we cannot make any rash decisions," Adelar said.

"And what of the Juarag, my king?" a female noble that Eva didn't recognize inquired from across the court. "How long before they begin raiding over the mountains into the heartland?"

"All of western Altaris must be united if we are to defeat the Smelterborn," the king said in a raised voice, discouraging further dissent. "Rhylance, Pandion, Maizoro, the Scrawls, and yes, even the Juarag. I will send a delegation to meet with their warchiefs and form an alliance against the Smelterborn."

Although none of them spoke, Eva saw that many of the nobility thought their king had gone mad judging by the looks on their faces. When the Smelterborn invaded the Endless Plains, the tribes of the cat people began a mass exodus in the only direction possible: west, toward Rhylance. The Juarag and their vicious sabercats had pillaged the eastern frontier of Rhylance for decades. Now they weren't raiding anymore, they were conquering, fighting for their very existence. Eva didn't think even the threat of Smelterborn could bridge the gap of malice between the two races. Still, it sounded better to Eva than waging war on two fronts at once, and she wondered why more of the nobility didn't realize that. Caught up in her own thoughts on the matter, Eva almost missed the king's next statement.

"The peace delegation will be led by my niece."

Eva felt the color drain from her face and her stomach drop to the hard stone floor as all eyes turned to her.

Then again, maybe an alliance with the Juarag wasn't such a good idea after all.

Chapter
2

"The Juarag only respect strength," Adelar said. It was hours after the council ended and the two of them sat in the king's private study. "I've pushed the nobles far enough with this proposal — if I suggested I go myself, they would lose their heads."

Eva pouted. "Send Andor!"

Adelar shook his head. "The lord commander cannot declare war or negotiate peace treaties. We must abide by our laws."

"Why not one of the nobles, then?" Eva asked, head still spinning. "Any of them would be a better representative for Rhylance than me!"

Adelar placed both hands on her shoulders and looked into her bright blue eyes with his own.

"Eva, listen to me," he said. "The last thing most of the nobles want is peace with the Juarag — they'd rather see us burn to the ground if it means the Juarag would be slaughtered as well. A strong king knows when he must bend to prevent himself from breaking. Your grandfather taught me that."

"But why me?"

Beckoning for Eva to follow, Adelar passed through the doors of his chambers into the empty court. On the wall behind the throne, a long banner hung, listing all of the rulers of Rhylance since the

Sorondarans first landed on Altaris' shore hundreds of years before. The king pointed to the bottom. Below Eva's grandparents, Adelar, and Andor a new piece of fabric had been sewn in with her father's name on it, replacing the spot where he'd been removed when exiled.

Below that…Eva saw her own name.

"You're not just the last heir of our house," Adelar said in a quiet voice from behind Eva. "When I die, you will become Queen of Rhylance and sit on the Winged Throne."

Eva felt her mouth go dry and she tried to swallow hard, tried to breathe — tried to do anything but stare in shock.

"I…I don't…"

It was beyond comprehending. The Queen of Rhylance? For more than three-quarters of her life, she'd just been a simple smith's apprentice in the craftsman district of Gryfonesse. Becoming Windsworn had seemed far-fetched enough. Eva realized she was babbling but couldn't think of an intelligent response, let alone speak it.

Adelar laughed. It didn't make her feel any better.

"No one is ever really prepared to rule, but if you're lucky and I'm careful, you won't have to worry about it for a long time," he said. "Still, it's high time you started learning some of these things and experience is the best teacher. Do you understand now?"

Eva focused hard on keeping her dinner from spewing all over the family tapestry. Her heart pounded louder than a Juarag war drum. "What if I mess up?" she managed at last. "What if I say the wrong thing or I can't persuade them or — ?"

"You won't," her uncle said in a voice that offered no room for argument. "I couldn't ask for a more worthy successor. I'm proud of the woman you've become and… and I know your father was as well."

A rush of emotion overwhelmed Eva and she looked at the ground. The loss of her father was still a gaping wound that refused to scar over. At the same time, she felt a rush of pride in herself and a determination to succeed.

"I'll do my best."

Hours later, Eva left the royal palace. Her head buzzed with all sorts of advice about controlling the tone of her voice, holding her body to convey strength without seeming haughty and a hundred other things a good diplomat should know. The rest of the courtyard was deserted save for Fury, her blood red gryphon. Her fellow riders were gone — no doubt they'd returned with Andor to the Windsworn's mountain headquarters, the Gyr.

Eva reached Fury's side and absentmindedly ran a hand down his head feathers and across the gryphon's back to his short, copper-colored fur. Her brain spun in tired circles, trying to make sense of the day. Although it had only been a few days since she'd returned with Sigrid, Chel, and Ivan from her search for her father, Eva felt like a lifetime had passed. She swung into Fury's saddle and strapped into her leg harness before clicking her tongue for the gryphon to take off.

In spite of the day's stress, a smile spread across Eva's face when Fury gathered his powerful feline hind legs, reared back and launched them into the air. Rising higher and higher above Gryfonesse, Eva let out a long sigh of happiness and reveled in the freedom of the open air.

Deep winter crept across Rhylance. In spite of the cold and bitter winds whipping at Eva, she still felt more at ease than she had in weeks. Looking over Fury's side at the shrinking white marble buildings, markets stalls, and insect-sized people, she found it hard to believe she'd ever dreaded flying. Now, instead of a death sentence, it was her escape.

Soaring wide, away to the west of the Gyr, Eva and Fury passed over fallow farm fields and woodlands blanketed in a mantle of snow. Above the trees, life stood still. Gray clouds drifted through a forlorn winter sky, ushering silence for miles in every direction.

It wasn't until the Gyr shrank in the distance to a speck the size of Eva's thumb that she turned back. By now, her cheeks were nipped with the cold and her hands felt numb, even through her gloves and furs. As Fury soared back over the same quiet expanse they'd just crossed, Eva let her mind drift to a roaring fireplace inside the mountain, mulled cider and perhaps a long dip in the hot pools deep within the cavernous rock of the Gyr.

Yet the burdens of the recent days returned with each mile. Eva's mind drifted from the threat of the upcoming Smelterborn, Seppo's revelation and, most importantly, the task her uncle had given her.

The mountain drew closer, its crags and broken edges swathed in stubborn drifts of snow. Fury wheeled around to the southern side of the mountain, still climbing higher and higher. Eva squinted and huddled closer down against the gryphon's body, a shiver running through her. When at last the Roost appeared and Fury glided onto the smooth rock floor of the cavern, Eva's enjoyment of cold solitude was long gone.

After rubbing down and feeding Fury, Eva wandered through the halls. It was early evening, a time between training and dinner when most of the Gyr's inhabitants would be in their rooms, relaxing, washing or studying before the evening meal. Eva made her way to the kitchen, grabbing a bowl of stew and a hunk of hearty dark bread before the dinner rush. Although she passed a number of familiar faces and said hello, she felt no desire to join the hustle and bustle of the Main Hall. Instead, she returned to her quarters and found them empty.

Sigrid, she guessed, would be down in the hot pools or making her way to dinner. Eva enjoyed her meal and the prolonged alone time without her bunkmate, not thinking much of anything as she spooned chunks of stew into her mouth. After cleaning the bowl with the heel of her bread she contemplated going to the library and curling up by the fire or heading to bed early. A knock interrupted the decision.

Opening the door, Eva found Tahl looking back at her. In the whirlwind of her return, they'd only had a few spare moments to spend together. Eva felt a sudden rush of guilt for not seeking him out when she'd returned.

"Oh," she said, mind suddenly blank. When Eva deserted the Windsworn to go look for her father, she'd asked Tahl to come with her. He hadn't.

And now, here they were, together in body but with all the miles Eva had traveled between their relationship.

He hadn't changed a bit, Eva reflected. Still the same collected, self-assured Tahl, leaning against the door frame like he wasn't meant to be anywhere else in the world.

"You're a hard person to track down," he said. A small, thin smile told Eva he wasn't really joking.

"I don't mean to be." When he didn't say anything, she tried again. "Do you want to come in?"

Tahl raised a bottle wrapped in cloth and jerked his head down the hall. "I've got a better idea. Grab a blanket."

Eva knew what he had in mind: their secret spot on a ledge overlooking the city. Between the conversation with her uncle and the cold flight, Eva hardly wanted to leave the comfort of her room. But instead of insisting they stay in, Eva found herself grabbing a blanket.

Outside, they settled down on the cold stone. A shiver ran through Eva, as much from the feel of Tahl's arms wrapping around her as the cold. She realized the last time they'd been there together was the night before she'd freed Chel from the dungeon and sneaked away with Sigrid and Ivan by cover of darkness.

"I missed this." Now that they were there and the blanket started to warm her, Eva was glad she'd come.

"I missed you."

Tahl leaned forward and kissed her on the cheek.

Eva felt another rush of warmth and twisted around to face him. "You missed."

They both snorted at the weak joke and kissed again.

For a long time after, neither spoke. They contented themselves staring down at the twinkling lights of Rhylance's capital, Gryfonesse, below and sipping Tahl's mulled cider.

"Things are going to change around here."

Eva could only nod in agreement. Tahl had no idea and she didn't feel like ruining the night with more talk about war and politics and responsibility. But as they sat there longer, the feeling gnawed away at Eva until she could ignore it no longer.

"I have to tell you something."

"Hmm?"

She told Tahl about the council, the First Forge and, most importantly, her appointment to Princess of Rhylance.

"I've only got one question," Tahl said when Eva finished. "Is the appropriate title your grace, your eminence or most exalted princess?"

Eva turned around and punched his shoulder. "Oh, ha-ha." She pretended to pout, then added in a soft voice, "Your grace is preferable."

Tahl laughed and pulled her tighter, sending Eva's heart fluttering. "A thousand pardons, your grace," he said. "I guess, I should have realized...should have known."

"Known what?" Eva said. After the laughter faded, he'd grown aloof again. She turned around, pulling away from Tahl's arms to get a read on his face.

"Well..." Eva could feel him shifting uncomfortably against her. And then it dawned on Eva and she realized she was an idiot.

"You know I love you, what does me being heir to the throne have to do with anything?"

"Because," Tahl said, "you're going to be queen someday and I'm just...just some farm boy who happened to become a gryphon rider and happened to luck out at being good at fighting and flying."

Eva snorted. Everyone in the Gyr knew Tahl was one of the most skilled Windsworn in years — maybe since Aleron, her father. By comparison, Eva's skills as a rider made her look like a duck trying to pass as an eagle.

"Certainly the almighty Tahl, the golden boy of the Gyr isn't being self-conscious right now, is he?" she asked, laughing.

"I'm serious!" Tahl gave her a soft, exasperated shove. "Blood matters with these things. And mine's about as common as it comes!"

Eva cupped his face in her hands and pulled him in for a long kiss. "That doesn't matter to me," she whispered when they parted. She drew in a quick breath to stop her head from spinning.

"Marry me."

The spinning stopped.

Eva stared. She searched for something, anything, but her mind wouldn't form the words. Instead, she kissed Tahl again.

"Is that a yes?" Tahl asked, grinning when they pulled apart.

"No," Eva said. "Because you haven't asked me yet!"

"Evelyn, Princess of Rhylance and heir to the Winged Throne, will you marry me, your grace?"

Eva didn't think about armies of Smelterborn and Juarag warriors. She didn't think about being the princess. She didn't think about anything but one word.

"Yes! YES!"

Chapter

3

"Just relax," Tahl said for the hundredth time.

"*I. Am. Relaxed,*" Eva replied through gritted teeth.

Behind her, Sigrid snorted. "You two are like a couple of old married folks, snapping at each other and mumbling under your breath."

Eva flinched but otherwise ignored the jibe. She and Tahl had agreed to keep the news of their engagement between the two of them for the time being until they at least had a moment to break the news to her uncles. Although she knew Sigrid couldn't possibly have any idea, the errant comment struck close to home. Eva tried to ignore the pinching in her stomach and focused on the figures approaching from the Juarag camp off in the distance.

This was their fourth stop and the fourth tribe she'd reached out to for peace talks. After almost a week of flying through the snow and camping in the cold, Eva had no idea what they had to show for it. Winter had left the Juarag ill-prepared to face the bitter western chinooks blowing down from the Windswept mountains on their way across the Endless Plains.

Each camp looked the same: a scattering of hide tents cased in ice, leaning from the drifts piled against their poles. The people looked worse: half-starved, haggard and desperate. The sabercats they saw were as lean as their riders. More than once, Eva thought the hungry beasts would attack the gryphons, desperate as they looked for fresh meat. Half-eaten carcasses proved they had no aversion to eating their own kind given the chance.

The awful weather impeded their progress more than anticipated. Most of the tribes were within a couple day's flight of one another at most, but each group answered to a separate chieftain. No one could give her a count before she left Rhylance but Eva guessed there were close to a dozen different warchiefs in all. The lack of central leadership made her diplomatic mission even more prolonged and stressful.

So far, two had agreed to King Adelar's terms while another remained undecided. The most recent, a giant of a woman riding a black and gray-streaked sabercat, would accept peace if Rhylance would feed them for the winter followed by an annual tribute of gold and weapons. Wide-eyed, Eva told the warchief she would have to speak with the king before she could make any such arrangement. She had no idea what the woman would have done had Eva told the Juarag no outright.

Rumor had it that the chieftain they were meeting with today, however, had influence over the entire council of warchiefs. Chel said his name was Arapheem. His tribe was the largest of the Juarag — the most warriors and the most sabercats. Chel believed if they could convince Arapheem to join their cause, the reluctant tribes would fall in line as well.

The Juarag's reaction to Chel was cool at best. Marked as an outcast — which they called Juarag-Vo — some openly spat on the ground at the sight of her, even if they begrudgingly showed her respect due to her place among the gryphon riders. One warchief had offered to provide Eva with a new translator, explaining in broken Westernese that Chel was unfit for such a role. Certainly, aside from knowing the language, Chel provided them with no diplomatic advantages.

Eva suppressed a shiver as a gust of wind rose up, swirling snow around them. Another gust cleared the flurries between her party and the Juarag. Arapheem looked the part of a mighty Juarag warchief. His dark brown sabercat's muscles bulged against its scarred hide.

The man wore a thick buffalo robe and half the hair on his head was shaved away. Orange war paint covered his face in sharp contrast to his earthy skin. Mounted warriors on full-grown sabercats flanked their chieftain, fully armed and scowling. Eva shivered again when she spotted a pair of shamans trailing behind the party — a man and a woman scarred and tattooed with runes. The white paint daubed on their heads made them look like skulls.

Behind her, Ivan cursed as the pair drew near. She knew the Scrawls had no love for the Juarag shamans — users of rune magic who, it was rumored, dabbled in blood magics and other dark sorcery. Whereas the Scrawls retained some of the knowledge of the ancient Palantines after the collapse of their civilization, the Juarag's magic hearkened back to older, darker, and wilder eras.

To show their peaceful intent, Eva insisted the gryphons remain a few dozen paces behind them, close enough to aid them if the Juarag proved treacherous but far enough away not to be construed as a threat. Arapheem, on the other hand, had no such reservations. His sabercat sauntered closer until its snarling, battered muzzle and yellowed, dagger-length teeth were within an arm's reach of Eva's face. She'd been this close to a sabercat before — it'd done it's best to eat her and she had no desire to repeat the experience. Although she shook in her boots, Eva forced her fears into the hard, frozen ground and held her place, fists clenched.

Avoiding the menacing feline eyes of the sabercat, Eva looked up at Arapheem. A long moment passed before his shoulders lifted in a small shrug and he jumped off his mount. Chel took her place at Eva's side as the warchief drew even with them and held his hand out in front of him, palm down in the traditional greeting.

Eva did the same, holding her hand, even with Arapheem's. Satisfied, the warchief waved his sabercat away. With a reluctant snarl, the enormous feline took a few steps and returned to the group of warriors and shamans standing watch a few paces from their leader.

"Greetings, Arapheem, mighty chief of the Juarag," Eva said in a loud, clear voice. Her legs might've been quaking but she forced herself to sound calm and collected.

Chel started to repeat the message in the Juarag tongue until the warchief halted her with his hand. "There is no need. Let us speak in your tongue, Eva-lyn Bloodrider."

Bloodrider. She didn't know how the moniker had spread so swiftly among the Juarag but that was what they called her, the rider of the blood-colored gryphon. Eva did her best to hide her surprise at the man's near perfect use of her own language. The warchief seemed to notice regardless. "We are not all the mindless savages you would paint us out to be."

"I apologize for my ignorance," Eva said. "You honor me with the use of our words — perhaps one day, I will speak your tongue as well as you do mine."

Arapheem gave a thin smile. "Perhaps one day, all sky people will speak our tongue, eh?"

The threat was hard to miss. Eva heard grumbling behind her, and guessed someone — Sigrid, most likely — had reached for their weapon. Across from her, the Juarag's hands drifted to their own clubs, spears, and swords.

"Perhaps, but today we are here to discuss peace, not war," Eva said. She glanced backward and shot a glare at Sigrid who froze halfway through drawing her ax. "Neither of our languages will be spoken if the Smelterborn kill us all."

"The iron giants." Arapheem spat on the frozen earth at his feet. "They are a curse upon this land."

"They must be stopped," Eva agreed. "In this, we have a common cause."

"They must be stopped," Arapheem nodded, "but that does not mean the sky people are not our enemies too."

"It doesn't have to be that way," Eva said, hoping the sudden anxiety she felt at the chieftain's tone wasn't apparent in her voice. "The Juarag are trapped between the hammer and the anvil. What does it accomplish to fight two wars at once?"

"Do you not think us up to the task?" The warchief swept a hand behind him at his warriors, who straightened a little on the backs of their sabercats, poking out their chests and raising their chins

"Perhaps we should break the hammer now? What do you say to that, Bloodrider? The Smelterborn might not be a worry to us if we sat inside your stone walls.

"I do not doubt the strength of the Juarag," Eva said. "But you face not only Rhylance but Pandion, Maizoro and the Scrawls as well. Even if you were to defeat our combined armies, the Smelterborn would still be waiting and who would be left to fight them? Is Altaris not big enough for all of us to live in peace once the iron giants are gone?"

Arapheem's eyes narrowed. "You tell me, Bloodrider. It was your people who came over the western mountains in the days of my grandfathers and drove us east. Any blood we have shed since was only to reclaim what was rightfully ours."

Eva knew she was flying in rough skies. Arapheem was testing her. With the right words, she could still win him over. Say something wrong and there would be blood then and there. It all hinged on what she chose to say next.

"The raiding of our outposts and the driving of your people away from the foothills are both in the past," Eva said, trying to put some stone in her voice. "We can argue about who has killed who the most or we can work together to defeat the Smelterborn. The golems do not care if it is winter or summer, how cold it is or how deep the snow falls. They will keep coming. Together, we can defeat them."

"These are lies," one of the shamans growled from beside his war cat. "The sky people think they can trick us. They —"

Arapheem held up a hand and the other man fell silent.

"What would it benefit us to trick you?" Eva said. "If we wanted to see the Juarag destroyed, we would leave you to the weather and the Smelterborn."

"What is this way of defeating the iron giants?" Arapheem asked. "How is it done?"

Eva hesitated. Had she succeeded or was this still a test?

"My uncle, King Adelar of Rhylance, asks you to join us at council, in three week's time. He would also ask that you use your influence among the other Juarag tribes to convince them to do the same. I have spoken with some and not all understand reason."

"Hmm," Arapheem looked past Eva, up at the peaks of the Windswepts in the distance. "How will I assure the other chieftains this is not a trap?"

"We will meet at Eagle's Point," Eva said, pointing to a cluster of mountains shooting off from the main body of the Windswepts. "In the ruins, on neutral ground. To show his good faith, the king has agreed to send blankets and additional supplies to any tribe who would have them."

"Your uncle is a desperate man," Arapheem said, "to give so much without any guarantee in return."

"The king is a trusting man," Eva said. "And in the face of complete destruction, what other course is there to take?"

"You have my word the Earthfang tribe will honor this agreement," Arapheem said. "But I cannot speak for the other warchiefs until a council is held."

Eva nodded. "I understand. We will return in two week's time for their answer. Will that allow you to get word to them?"

"It will be done," Arapheem said. He stretched out his hand and he and Eva grasped forearms. She fought to keep her hand clenched. The man's grip made her arm and fingers tingle from the pressure. "I am honored by your visit, Bloodrider. I will do what I can to make this alliance so."

Eva fought back the urge to sigh, laugh or cry all at once. Instead, she gave a curt nod, releasing her grip first, as was polite. "We will meet soon."

Walking away, Eva felt like her legs were cherry-red metal bars, ready to buckle at any moment. Back at their gryphons, Sigrid slapped her on the back, and Ivan and Chel offered their congratulations.

"Looks like you were cut out for this diplomatic business after all," Tahl said, giving her a one-armed hug.

Eva smiled. A small measure of relief settling over her as she climbed into Fury's saddle. Deep down, however, she knew the struggle had only begun.

Chapter 4

The wind howled around the rocks of Eagle's Point, driving biting snow at Eva's cheeks and nose, the only areas not protected by thick furs. The Point, which appeared to have been a lookout post of some sorts in ages past, had little to offer in way of protection. The remaining rings of broken stones poked through the drifts like cracked, rotted teeth.

"The Scrawls believe this was once a site of power, used to observe the movement of the stars, sun, and moon throughout the seasons." Ivan's voice sounded muffled behind a thick scarf wrapped around the lower part of his face.

"I don't give a flying feather about this hole, even if the sky-cursed First Forge is buried beneath all this snow," Sigrid snapped. Ice crusted her eyelids and the tips of her spiky dark hair protruding from her hood. "And I'm tired of all this talking, especially when I have to freeze my ass off to listen to it. Let's fight the Smelterborn already and stop babbling on about it!"

The gryphons were as miserable and irritated as Sigrid, snapping at one another beneath a coat of sleet frozen to their fur. Eva had to agree. They'd counseled and debated long enough. She hoped the Juarag were miserable enough to keep the negotiations short — and agreeable.

Regardless of the foul weather, the two parties boasted an array of people the likes of which Eagle's Point had probably never seen. In addition to the lord commander and dozens of Windsworn, King Adelar attended with his own wing of gryphon riders pledged to his defense.

Tahl numbered among them, chosen by the king to be among his honor guard for the occasion. Eva saw him now, standing across the large flat space of rock, hooded cloak drawn over his head, hands on the hilt of his sword, scanning for danger. In spite of the added worry his position caused her, she couldn't help but feel a surge of pride watching him among the other elite riders. Still, she would have preferred him by her side, if nothing else, to provide some added warmth.

The high mountain passes from Rhylance were buried in deep snow, meaning all attendees from the western side of the Windswepts had to be flown in. In addition to the twenty or so Sorondarans, there were also a half-dozen Scrawl Elders who had been fit enough to make the freezing journey over the mountains to represent their peoples.

A handful of delegates from Pandion and Maizoro came as well. Each shivered in their furs and robes, unused to the biting cold of the mountains compared to the temperate coast and northlands from which they hailed. Eva couldn't imagine a place more different from the mild coasts and sun-drenched farmlands than the bleak rock of Eagle's Point.

Although Eva felt half-frozen herself, she was glad she'd even been able to attend. Since openly naming her as the heir, both Adelar and Andor had watched — or had someone watch— Eva's every step. She knew it was for her protection but suspected it was so she didn't try run off on another wild journey, too. She'd begged them to allow her to come to Eagle's Point, arguing that she'd orchestrated the meeting in the first place and deserved to see how it played out.

Her uncles relented, but only on the condition that a personal guard accompanied her. The group was comprised of two members of the King's Wing — not Tahl, unfortunately — two members of the Lord Commander's Wing — of which Sigrid was one, fortunately —

and a handful of others, chosen by Eva. Which of course meant Ivan, Chel, and Wynn. When Wynn asked, Eva almost told her no, until she realized she was treating the younger girl the same way her two uncles treated her.

Eva hid a smile, watching Wynn stare wide-eyed around the gathering. A horn pealed from the edge of the rock circle. In the swirling snow, Eva had a hard time making out the source. She knew what the sound meant though: the Juarag had arrived.

Hands tightened on weapons and faces grew tense. A few minutes later, Eva saw the dark, hulking shapes of sabercats padding across the snow. The silence of their approach made it all the more unsettling. There were fifty or so in all, their lithe bodies painted for war. The wet snowfall caused the beasts' markings to trickle down their sides, dripping reds, blues, purples, oranges and green into the snow, like a bleeding rainbow. A man out front — Arapheem, Eva guessed by the look of his war cat — called a halt a bow shot from the western delegates.

As the Juarag crested the hill on foot, Eva started forward, ignoring the protests of her guard who followed close behind. The Juarag riders dismounted and left their snarling sabercats on the edge of the Point. Even with the distance between the cats and the gryphons watching from the crags and rock of the cliff face behind her, Eva could almost feel the mutual hatred between the two magnificent animal breeds. Humans aside, she doubted it would take much to start a fight between the gryphons and sabercats.

"Hail Arapheem, mighty chieftain of the Juarag," King Adelar said when the party drew close enough to hear his words over the moaning winds. Eva took a place beside her uncles and the Scrawl Elders.

"It is good weather to talk about the ending of days," Arapheem said, glancing up at the swollen, snow-filled skies and grinning. When he looked back at them, the warchief held out his hand to Eva in the same gesture as the first time they'd met. Without bothering to check for permission from the king, Eva stepped forward and returned the greeting.

"I have brought the Juarag chiefs as you asked, Bloodrider,"

Arapheem said to her. "Now tell us how we may defeat the Smelterborn."

This time, Eva deffered. "My uncle, King Adelar of Rhylance, will tell you our plan for battle."

Adelar began a long talk about the importance of uniting against the Smelterborn. As he spoke, Eva studied the other Juarag chiefs. None of the women accompanying Arapheem looked especially glad to be there. Most wore unconcealed scowls while they listened to Arapheem confer with the king. Some studied the rest of the delegation and the gryphons, no doubt sizing up their opponents should the gathering turn into a fight. One man, an older warrior with hair black as coal and a milky-white left eye, stared at Eva. His gaze fell on her as cold and devoid of life as the snow-drenched mountains around them.

He reminded Eva of Uthred, the second-in-command of the Windsworn and her uncle Andor's right-hand man. When Eva had first come to the Gyr to begin her training, he'd ordered Sigrid — who, at the time, harbored a deep resentment for Eva — to beat her into a pulp in the sparring circle. For most of her first year, Eva thought Uthred was trying to kill her. Instead, in his own harsh way, he had tempered her resolve, and made Eva earn everything she got, even as the rider of the fabled red gryphon.

In the years since, Eva developed a begrudging respect for the hard, gray warrior. She sensed the black-haired Juarag chief across from her was just as hard, but without any of the moral limitation or sense of honor that reined in Uthred. As Arapheem and the king spoke in earnest about how an alliance might work and how a grand attack on the Smelterborn could be accomplished, Eva forced herself to meet the man's good eye.

"I cannot just give you the eastern frontier," Adelar said after a lengthy exchange. "I'm aware that it was once Juarag lands, but that was hundreds of years ago. My people have built settlements there —"

"Juarag are there now," Arapheem said. "Settlements are gone. All your people fled over the mountains. That is where they should stay."

As apparent as a shift in the wind, Eva felt the negotiations take a turn for the worse.

"Are you threatening me?"

Arapheem let the king's word blow away before he shrugged. "Juarag chieftains do not threaten. We only promise."

Several members of the western delegation muttered in discontent. Their discontent seemed to fuel the king's resolve even further. Likewise, the Juarag chiefs behind Arapheem toyed with their weapons.

"Need I remind you that your people are at our mercy?" Adelar said, voice rising and hardening. "The Smelterborn will crush you against the Windswepts if you choose to fight us both. There will be no Juarag left to claim the frontier."

"Then maybe we will come for you, instead," Arapheem said. "Your mountains and snow will not be enough to stop us sky-king."

"Stop!"

Eva jumped between her uncle and Arapheem. "The Smelterborn are who we must fight, not one another! If we do not work together, only golems will live on the frontier."

For a long moment, both her uncle and Arapheem stared at Eva, neither speaking. The wind howled a forlorn note through the mountains. Everyone hung on what would be said next.

A black flash passed the corner of Eva's eye, close enough for her to feel the whisk of the cold metal before the large iron javelin struck the frost-bitten stones and skittered away. A moment later, several more javelins filled the air, striking Juarag and westerner alike.

"Treachery!" Arapheem shouted, drawing his sword.

The two parties might have slaughtered one another if Eva hadn't spotted the dark shapes darting between the rocks off the edge of the Point.

"No!" she said, pointing. "Smelterborn!"

Swift, dark, metal forms leaped from cover, hefting more javelins. Shouts of alarm erupted from both sides. Eva spun and found Smelterborn surrounding them on all sides. These were a new make she'd never see before — smaller and leaner like the scout golems, but heavily armed like their bigger, slower counterparts.

"Protect the king and the princess!"

Tahl and both guard parties rushed to shield Eva and the king but Eva pushed away.

"They need me!" she said, drawing her father's sword. The runes on the blade flashed pale blue in the gray light of the day.

Before anyone could stop her, Eva joined the fray. The complete chaos of her first pitched battle nearly stopped her in her tracks. There appeared to be only twenty to thirty of the smoke-colored Smelterborn, but each fought with the ferocity of ten men. Gryphons screamed and dropped like arrows from the sky. Juarag raiders, Sorondaran knights, Windsworn and Scrawl rune mages fell like trees beneath an iron avalanche

"Aim for the eyes!" Eva shouted as a burst of flame shot from the hands of nearby Scrawl. She knew their magic might be the only thing to turn the tide. "Aim for the eyes — it's the only way to bring them down!"

In the chaos, she wasn't sure anyone heard her. To her left, a man screamed as he flew through the air before smashing into two of his fellow soldiers. Eva pushed her way forward, ignoring her friends' shouts for her to stop. A Smelterborn loomed out of the blizzard in front of her.

Pushing aside her terror, Eva summoned her training. The Smelterborn swung at her with a sword the size of a lance. Eva raised her weapon and braced to parry the blow. Aleron's rune-inscribed blade cut through the golem's weapon. The Smelterborn registered no surprise or shock at having his sword cut in two. Instead, it tossed the hilt aside and raised its shield in both hands, then charged.

Eva dove to the side and shifted the grip on her sword. She swung hard sideways and sparks filled the air as the blade scored the iron face of the shield. Pivoting with the momentum of her swing, Eva severed the golem's arm at its elbow. But the Smelterborn registered no pain. With its remaining hand, it hefted its shield overhead in a crushing blow.

Eva stumbled backward and lost her footing. She looked up just as the Smelterborn's shield swung toward her. She gritted her teeth. So this was how it would end.

At the last moment, a figure collided with the falling shield, forcing the edge inches to the right of Eva's head. Tahl rebounded off the shield and hit the ground hard. Scrambling, Eva swung low and severed the golem's leg. The Smelterborn toppled over backward. Before it could recover, Eva buried her blade in its armored chest.

An all-too-familiar bone-chilling wail split the air and a dark shape shot out of the ruined helmet, like a streak of black tar in the snow-filled sky. Eva ran to Tahl's side as he stood, using his shield to steady himself. The tumult of the battle around them faded into the back of Eva's mind as she searched him for any serious wounds. A relieved sob tore from her chest upon finding him okay.

"Gonna be…sore tomorrow," he grunted.

"I had it handled," Eva said and they shared a grim laugh.

Pushing her soaked hair out of her face, Eva saw about two-thirds of the Smelterborn were down, although the humans' superior numbers wore thin. Not far off, Sigrid, Iva, Wynn, and Chel toppled another Smelterborn after a blast of Ivan's ice kenning struck it in the head. When they joined Eva and Tahl, the Scrawl bent over, hands on his knees like he'd just ran up the mountainside.

"Everyone alright?" Eva asked them.

"No thanks to you," Sigrid said, hefting her notched ax. She grinned. "I'm supposed to be the one who rushes into a fight without thinking it through."

Chel held a broken spear in her hand and nodded. Wynn only stared, face as pale as the snow.

"Wynn," Eva said, seized by concern. "Are you okay?"

Before she could answer, Ivan, bent over again and spewed his breakfast at their feet.

"Sorry," he muttered, wiping his mouth with the back of his hand.

The westerners and the Juarag fought side by side as a wall of weapons and shields, herding the remaining golems toward the cliffs. Shouting and screaming, the unlikely allies drove the band of golems off the edge. Only two Smelterborn remained. Both charged the king and Arapheem. Once again, Eva charged forward, leaving her friends to follow.

The first golem fell beneath a blast of fire from a Scrawl kenning. The last, instead of retreating from the lost battle, went berserk. The Smelterborn hit the first wave of knights, armor smashing into armor as it abandoned its weapon, tossing the men and women aside with both hands. Nearby Juarag sprinted to the defense of their war leader and were crushed beneath the golem's iron fists.

A shot of ice hit the Smelterborn in the shoulder sending it spinning. Faster than Eva could blink, the golem recovered as if the defeat of its fellow somehow added to its strength and speed. Several kennings hit the golem all at once, a storm of ice, fire, wind, and earth. The Smelterborn absorbed each blow, in turn, wading through the rune magic. More soldiers died as they crossed in front of its path.

Although nothing could stop it, the golem's progress slowed just enough. Eva struck. Her overhead slash cut deep, leaving a gaping line of heated metal curling back on itself. Dropping to its knees, the golem continued to crawl forward and a horrifying, guttural chant filled the air.

Eva screamed and swung down again with all of her might. A blast of ice struck the Smelterborn's helmet. It didn't stop crawling. Summoning the last of her strength, Eva raised her sword in both hands and drove it through the back of the golem's head. The dark spirit trapped within burst free, knocking everyone within an arm's length of the Smelterborn to the ground. The now-empty suit of armor gave a last twitch and lay still.

"Nothing would stop it," Arapheem said in a hushed voice. "When we killed the others, it only grew stronger."

Adelar could only stare at the smoking hole in the golem's helm.

The two leaders tore their eyes from the horrific sight and grasped hands. All around them, Juarag and westerner alike stood in shock and exhaustion, any thought of battle amongst themselves forgotten.

"We will fight this evil together," Arapheem said.

King Adelar nodded. "Together."

Chapter 5

In the coming weeks, Eva's remaining hopes of resuming a normal, quiet routine were squashed. After the council at Eagle's Point, both the Gyr and Gryfonesse transformed into a night and day war machine. Riders flew constantly from the mountains, scouting the advancing Smelterborn horde or ferrying supplies and men over the mountain passes of the Windswepts whenever the snows allowed. Builders worked tirelessly to assemble fortifications and choke points in the high passes in anticipation of the arrival of the golems.

The winter proved to be a double-edged sword. While it slowed the Smelterborn and allowed more time for preparation, the defenders constantly battled the snow and cold, especially in the heart of the Windswepts. But the deep of winter passed, and hints of spring appeared in the lowlands. Instead of providing comfort, however, the tiny buds on trees and clumps of grass poking through the rotting snow reminded Eva that they were running out of time.

A hodgepodge of carts and sleds fought through the sopping mud, melting drifts and dirty spring runoff to climb the western side of the mountains where assembly on the fortifications continued. From a distance, the long lines of workers stretched up the foothills and into the passes like trails of ants.

For as many Sorondarans and other westerners that went east, hundreds of Juarag refugees came west. After tense negotiations with the nobles, the king and council placed the nomads in the fields to the south of the capital, saving the farmlands and orchards to the north for their crops, pastures, and orchards. Their arrivals were the old and very young, along with whoever among the men and women were not warriors. Arapheem had sworn no sabercats or raiders would be sent over the passes into Rhylance. Although he kept his word, whenever Eva visited Gryfonesse the city was tense, the citizens muttering about the "savages" at their gates. Eva found it borderline ridiculous that they were more worried about the half-starved Juarag refugees than the army of Smelterborn drawing closer with each passing hour.

In the hustle and bustle, Eva rarely saw any of her friends. Ivan worked on the front lines, using his rune magic to assist in building the mountain fortifications. Sigrid and Tahl stayed busy commanding wings of scouts on reconnaissance missions. As a member of the king's wing, Eva saw Tahl more than she would have otherwise, but it was never enough. She savored each moment they stole away together — mostly late at night when no one demanded their time elsewhere.

They still hadn't told anyone about their engagement. Whenever Eva thought she had a moment with Adelar, something always came up demanding the king's attention. She worried Tahl would be angry but they saw one another so little that neither wanted to waste time on anything but the moment they shared.

Chel served as an ambassador between the Juarag refugees and the king's council. She received little appreciation from either side. To the Juarag, Chel was an outcast, unclean and possessed by bad spirits. To Rhylance's nobles, she was no different than all the other warriors who had raided the frontier for years.

With as much time as Eva spent in Gryfonesse, she thought at least Soot and Seppo would have been around to visit. But the smith and golem were as busy as everyone else. The Scrawls continued to study the Dark Wonder and interview Seppo to glean every bit of information possible about the First Forge. The rest of the time, Soot and Seppo worked long hours in the forge, preparing tools and weapons for the coming war. As back-breaking and exhaustive as the labor was, Eva would have given anything to join them, to pretend just for a few hours she was just Eva, the smith's assistant.

Instead, she was Princess Evelyn, rider of the red gryphon and heir to the throne of Rhylance. She soon found the work behind the crown was much less glamorous than the title itself. For the most part, Eva sat in council after council as various leaders from across western Altaris plotted the progress of the Smelterborn and strategized the most probable routes they would take to cross the mountains.

The Windswepts stretched from the border of Maizoro in the north all the way to the land of the Scrawls in the south. Blocking all of the westward passes was impossible. Therefore, the plan was to bottleneck the Smelterborn into a handful of locations where their numbers and inhuman strength would count for less. It seemed like a good plan, but Eva worried what would happen if the Smelterborn simply chose another route.

Each day, additional fighting forces arrived from all over Altaris. Pandion — a coastal country inhabited by Sorondaran descendants — sent hundreds of soldiers and supplies through the milder Curtain Mountains to the west of Rhylance which were already clear of snow.

Scores of Scrawls, their carts, and beasts of burden painted with as many runes as their riders, poured in from the south. From the north, the Maizorans came with heavy wagons carrying corn, squash, beans and more — produce from a softer land that never felt the bite of winter cold. Eva had never seen so many different people from different places, not even during their brief stay in the Mother of Cities during its festival to the Ancestors.

As busy as her friends and loved ones were, Eva's days were filled with the most mundane tasks she could imagine. Instead of performing her regular Windsworn duties, such as flying on patrol, Eva was grounded in Gryfonesse attending to more princess-like endeavors. None of them offered any excitement or physical labor and made Eva want to scream and pull her hair out.

She lived for the few evening flights she was allowed with Fury and the rare duties that took her out of the citadel grounds into the rest of the city or surrounding countryside. Likewise, she longed for the days when she could fly patrol with Fury and her fellow riders or spend the night curled up with either a book or Tahl by the fires inside the Gyr's library.

And so it continued for weeks on end, as the last vestiges of winter disappeared and spring burst forth in all its glory. Even though war loomed life still went on: Rich, dark rows of earth lined the fields, a hundred different colors of flowering clover blanketed the pastures and the trees drooped, heavy with pregnant blossoms.

In spite of the stress of war and frustration of being a member of the royal family, Eva couldn't help but enjoy a day outside in the beautiful spring weather, overseeing another load of supplies being transported to the Juarag camp. Fury, Eva, and Chel sat on a small rise, watching the last wagons roll down the graveled road. Fury's copper feathers glistened in the burgeoning sun as the gryphon clawed at the soft earth with his foretalons, eager to be back in the sky. For a moment, Eva could almost convince herself she was just out on a noonday flight with Chel.

Despite everything they'd gone through to reach the valley, the Juarag refugees fared well over the winter. The nobles still grumbled about feeding "the savages" but thanks to Rhylance's allies, the storehouses had never been more full. A host of immortal golem's bent on total destruction might have been approaching, but at least there was plenty for everyone to eat.

Looking at each tribe's group of skin tents and cook fires, Eva reflected on how clean and organized the camps of the "savages" were. As far as she knew, there hadn't been any real disorder between the Rhylance teamsters and the Juarag, either. The nomads kept to themselves and seemed content to be left to themselves as much as possible.

Eva supposed it couldn't hurt that their hot-headed warriors were all far away in the mountains, preparing for battle. If they all somehow made it through the war, Eva wondered how smooth the Juarag's exodus from Rhylance would be when their chieftains and raiders reunited with their tribes.

She was about to mount Fury and leave when a ring of wagons on the edge of the Juarag camp caught her eye. They all featured small cabins built on top of their frames and the sound of tambourines and bells floated up from their midst. At the sound of the strange, wild music, a smile spread across Eva's face.

"Come on," she said, waving to Chel. "I think I know who that is!"

They hopped on Fury's back and made the short flight down the hill to the riverside camp. Landing, Eva saw several Juarag rush for their tents at the site of a gryphon so close, but the owners of the wagons waved and called out greetings. Stepping away from Fury, Eva and Chel met a middle-aged woman wearing large hoop earrings and her hair pulled back in a bright scarf.

"It *is* you!" Eva shouted, hugging the woman. "I am glad you and your people made it, Belka."

The woman smiled, bangles jingling on her wrists as she pulled out of the hug. "It is all thanks to you, Eva. We arrived just ahead of you — I confess I did not hope to see you alive again. Tell me, were you successful in your search?"

Both Eva and Chel grew a little somber. They'd met Belka on the Endless while searching for Chel's tribe and Eva's father. Although they'd eventually found both, none of those loved ones escaped the Smelterborn's advance alive.

"We did," Eva said, feeling her eyes well with tears and an all-too-familiar lump build in her throat. "Thank you, again, for your help. Without the supplies you gave us, I don't think we could have finished our journey."

Belka's eyes searched them and seemed to recognize their still-fresh hurt. She nodded. "Think nothing of it. I do not know where my people would be without you."

"Is there anything I can do for you?" Eva asked. "Do you need anything — food, blankets? I can find you lodging in the city if you want."

Belka laughed. "We are more at home here, with the Juarag, than inside your city. You have done plenty. Do not worry about us."

An overwhelming happiness seized Eva and she hugged Belka once more, grateful for a small bit of joy amidst the frantic war preparation. The feeling was short-lived.

The shadow of a gryphon passed overhead, the whoosh of wings moment later heralding its landing. Eva turned and her heart sank at the grave expression on the rider's face. She recognized the woman, a member of the king's wing named Tess.

"Princess Evelyn, your are wanted at the palace immediately."

"What's wrong, Tess?" Eva asked.

The rider looked over Eva's shoulder at Belka and her people but Eva nodded, assuring her it was safe to continue.

"The Smelterborn, your highness," Tess said. "They've…moved faster than anticipated."

Eva swallowed and the warmth she felt from reuniting with Belka drained from her. "How close are they?"

"We've got ten days if we're lucky."

Chapter 6

"Ten days?" Adelar said. "That's over a month ahead of when we expected them. How in the sky is that even possible?"

Andor shook his head. "I can't explain it," he said in a flat voice. "But I flew out and saw for myself yesterday. It's like something is spurring them on, they're traveling at almost twice their old pace now, even through the thick country in the foothills."

The lord commander tossed a bundle of parchments on the table and continued speaking while the king looked over the reports. "Their numbers are close to a thousand or so, including their scouts and those smoky looking ones that attacked us at Eagle's Point. The men have taken to calling them Shadowstalkers.

Oh good, Eva thought, *let's make them sound even more terrifying than they already are.* She walked around the table to read the reports over Adelar's shoulder but before she could get close enough the king threw them on the table, exasperated.

"We need more time!"

"What —" Eva started.

"I think we can buy a little," Andor assured the king, ignoring Eva. "There's quite a few piles of loose rock from fortifying the passes — Uthred had an idea. We can send a few wings at a time to drop them on the front lines of the Smelterborn. It might slow their advance.

Arapheem and his raiders will take a few shots at them as well."

"I —"

"And they're heading toward the Talon?" Adelar asked.

Andor nodded. "We caught a break there, that's the one thing going according to plan. Even with the Smelterborn's increased speed, we should still be ready. General Brachus has overseen the construction all winter and assures me the fortifications will hold."

Before Eva could speak further, Adelar gestured across the war table. In addition to a map, small carved pieces marked the current positions of their armies and the armies of their allies. "That would give us enough time to get the last companies from Pandion and the Scrawls in place."

Eva frowned and glared at her two uncles who carried on their conversation as if she'd melted into the wall. The king and lord commander might preach the importance of her learning things, but whenever the time for decisions came, it was like she didn't exist.

She sat in a chair while Adelar and Andor continued to outline their strategies, thinking how much more use she would have been at the Gyr. As before, neither of them spared her a moment's notice. When Andor left at last to begin mustering the Windsworn, Adelar finally turned his attention to Eva.

"You'll be in charge of Gryfonesse while I'm gone."

Eva felt her mouth go dry and stomach churn at the thought. The feelings were replaced by a burning anger when she realized her uncle meant to leave her behind.

"While you're gone where?"

"The Talon," Adelar said, gesturing to the map. "I must have a presence among the soldiers."

Eva jumped out of the chair and clenched her shaking hands into fists. "*I will not be left behind while my friends and family go off to war!*"

The king sighed and ran a hand through his short graying hair. "Eva…"

"No!" Eva shouted. "My place is with the rest of the Windsworn — with you and Andor. I'm tired of sitting around counting coins and whatever other busy work you think up for me."

"Eva, as the crown princess, you can't spend your days solely as a Windsworn rider," Adelar said. She opened her mouth to yell again but he cut her off with a raised hand. "You've got to learn how to rule a kingdom."

"I've got years to do that!"

A strange expression crossed Adelar's face. "I thought the same thing when I was your age," he said in a quiet voice. "And I hated it as much as you do now. While my brothers went off on wild adventures I stayed here and learned about diplomacy and trade."

"There wasn't an army of Smelterborn coming to kill everyone and burn everything down to the ground then," Eva pointed out.

Adelar's usually stern face parted in a wry smile. "No, which is why it's even more important that you stay safe. We took too many chances at Eagle's Point. That can't happen again."

Eva's anger and frustration fell to a simmer against her uncle's cold logic. But the thought of her friends — and last remaining family — risking their lives while she stayed behind twisted her insides into knots.

As if sensing her divided loyalties, Adelar placed both hands on his niece's shoulders. "If we lose the Talon, the city and the Gyr are our last defense. You'll get more than your fill of fighting then."

Eva gave a slow, reluctant nod, swallowing hard to fight down the tears. She tried not to think of Tahl, Sigrid, Ivan, Wynn, Andor and everyone else against the might of the Smelterborn.

"I... I'd like to spend a day or two at the Gyr and..."

She'd meant to finish with "say goodbye," but the thought of what that might mean was unbearable, especially with her father's death still fresh in her mind and heavy on her heart.

"I understand," Adelar said, his face softening. "What about this: the Talon is less than two day's flight away. Why don't you join us on our flight out? You can tour the defenses with me and attend the war council. How does that sound?"

Eva forced a smile on her face and agreed. If that was the best she could get then so be it. And who knew, maybe something would happen that would force her to remain at the Talon?

Adelar seemed to read her mind. "On one condition," he said. "You must return to Gryfonesse when I say. And your guard will remain with you at all times. Understood?"

Nodding, Eva took a deep breath. "Understood."

The king drew Eva into a long hug. "We'll get through this, I promise."

Although it didn't last nearly long enough, Eva relished the short flight she and Fury took from the capital to the Gyr. Without Chel, who'd already returned to the mountain with Wynn, it was the first time Eva and Fury had been alone in... she didn't know how long. As soon as they were in the air, Fury did his best to pull away from her suggested directions. When Eva gave the red gryphon an impatient nudge with her heel to turn him the other way, Fury let out a rebellious screech and veered off on his own path.

"Hey, bonehead, knock it off!" she shouted at the back of Fury's head. Eva was about to give him a harder dig in the side for ignoring her when she realized he'd been cooped up as well at the palace.

Even though Fury couldn't see it, Eva shook her head in exasperation and gave the gryphon his head.

Delighted to have full freedom in the warm afternoon skies, Fury swooped and soared, his aerial prowess on display. In spite of her previous impatience, Eva relaxed and enjoyed the bond with her gryphon as he performed flips, dives and several other aeronautic acrobatics. Once more, her worries seemed to blow away in the open air.

Fighting her own reluctance as much as Fury's, Eva finally turned them back toward the Gyr. Fury complied, only voicing a half-hearted cry in response to her directing. Nearing the Roost, stark reality returned. Dozens of gryphons and riders flew in and out of the large opening in the side mountain that served as a landing strip. The unusual activity was yet another mark of the impending war and a jarring reminder that life at home was not how Eva remembered it.

The mountain's interior buzzed with activity. After seeing Fury unsaddled, groomed and fed, Eva made her way down the long staircase from the Roost toward the Main Hall through the bustle of riders. Although she saw plenty of friendly faces, none of her closest friends were anywhere to be found.

Halfway to her destination, a strange sensation overcame her, causing Eva to stop in her tracks. The sounds of other Windsworn laughing and talking around her faded. She looked to her right and saw a narrow side passage empty of people. A tingling sensation ran from the nape of her neck down her back just looking down the dimly lit tunnel.

Unsure why, Eva turned down the passage.

As soon as she stepped out of the main corridor, the light and noise faded behind the first bend in the smaller passage. The crystal lanterns on the wall flickered and sputtered a pale green light. A gentle breeze blew down the tunnel carrying a stale, musty scent with it. Eva glanced back once, eager to find her friends but the hair-raising feeling overtook her once more and she carried on.

A faint remembrance grew with each step Eva took, although she couldn't ever remember going down this passage before. A gryphon's scream echoed down the hall and Eva stopped, goosebumps spreading across her arms. A memory tugged at her mind, just out of reach. Now completely resolved to follow the passage, Eva carried on.

The farther she went, Eva became aware of a faint tapping sound. Although the tunnel twisted and wound about like a snake, there were no offshoots. Eva increased her pace. All the while the steady tapping noise grew louder.

The passage made a sharp twist. In the dim light, Eva almost ran into the rock wall, skidding to a halt and throwing her hands out to stop her. And then, she knew where she was. Looking at the ground, she recalled a frustrated, lost girl chasing after an ill-mannered gryphon hatchling.

She knew what came next.

Rounding the corner with caution, Eva peered into the larger chamber before her and spotted an enormous black gryphon with blind, milky eyes. The beast reared on its back two lion's legs and clawed at the air, letting loose another piercing scream. Although she'd spent years around gryphons, Eva's heart pounded in her chest and fear gripped her.

"Well, well, well," a familiar, cracked voice said. "Look who came back for a visit."

As the black gryphon settled down on all fours, a terribly ancient man hobbled around the edge of the chamber. His skin was even more spotted and discolored than Eva remembered, but the old man's green eyes still held their sharpness.

"Lord Vyr," Eva said. "It's been a long time."

Chapter 7

Ha!" Lord Vyr grinned, his paper-thin skin peeling back to reveal rows of yellow, broken teeth. "What is long time to a fledgling like you? Still, we're glad for the company, by storm, aren't we, Basil?"

The black gryphon let out a low hiss, suggesting he was anything but grateful. Eva took a cautious step back — the last time she'd been here she'd sworn the ancient gryphon was going to eat her.

"Oh don't worry about him, my dear, he's just all worked up because he's going to miss the battle. Come on!"

Eva followed the old man around the corner of the chamber, keeping one eye on the black gryphon as she did. Although he looked to be as blind as a bat, Basil's head followed her every movement and Eva was grateful to duck out of his gaze into a smaller cave where the gryphon wouldn't fit.

When she saw the table, Eva stopped in her tracks. It looked as terrible as before, the jet-black surface carved with runes and stained with ancient blood. Eva realized she'd seen some of the same runes etched on the armor of the Smelterborn and the ebony of the table looked exactly like her father's Dark Wonder. Another shiver ran through her and she began to regret her decision.

"Don't stare, girl!" Lord Vyr snapped, beckoning her forward. Eva approached the table with more caution than she had with Basil.

"How —"

"That gryphon of yours, a red one, wasn't it? How's he? Too big for you to chase around like a kitten, I'll wager!"

"He's...well," Eva said, unable to take her eyes off the table. "What —"

Lord Vyr snapped his gnarled, arthritic fingers underneath her nose. "Pay attention! It's rude to ignore your host. And here we were thinking you had manners, girl. You didn't even bring any honey for sky's sake!"

"But the table!" Eva pressed, irritated at the erratic old man. "The runes!"

Lord Vyr nodded. "Well, you've got some sense at least. And when it comes down to it, sense is more important than manners in a woman — ha!"

Eva frowned not sure if she was being complimented or insulted. "I've seen them before."

"Of course you have, of course you have, fledgling." Lord Vyr nodded vigorously and his thin strands of white hair bobbed around his head like cobwebs. "The Gyr used to belong to the Ancients — don't they teach you these things? They weren't all as wonderful as they seemed — feathers, no — all sorts of vile blood magics to gain power or live forever. Nasty, nasty times. Nasty people, for the most part."

The withered man hissed the last words out through his cracked teeth, sounding much like his gryphon in the chamber behind them.

"The prophecy!" Eva said, surprising herself. She struggled to recall the words.

"The lion, the eagle, and the queen," Lord Vyr said, jabbing his crooked fingers at various runes carved into the table. "It's all there. Do you not remember? One who can stop the iron storm and turn back the breaking wind."

"I remember," Eva said, "but I still don't have any idea what it means."

Lord Vyr, gurgled and spat a mouthful of phlegm onto the floor. Eva grimaced — it'd only missed her boots by a finger's width. The old man studied the disgusting glob for a second and then look at Eva, blinking.

"The meaning is in the finding, fledgling," he said. "When it comes down to it, prophecies are only as good as the people or creatures in them. The rest is up to you."

"You don't make any sense at all," Eva said. She had enough stress and frustration without listening to the babblings of a cracked old relic.

Lord Vyr sighed and seemed to be just as impatient with her.

"Fear or greatness." Eva shivered and the words echoed in her mind from years ago, when she'd been a scared, lost girl with an angry gryphon chick that hated her. "I sense greatness in you, but there is still much fear."

Eva couldn't argue, although greatness sure didn't seem all that it was cracked up to be if her life was any indication.

"What will do you, Evelyn?" Lord Vyr said in a hushed tone. "What you will do when all hope seems lost and you find yourself alone in the darkness?"

A sudden fury rushed through Eva. "I'll fight!" she shouted, surprised at her sudden outburst. She was tired of losing control, tired of always being afraid. "I'll fight to the death!"

Lord Vyr nodded and bared his broken teeth in what was more of a snarl than smile.

"We've always liked your fire, girl," he said. "Even when you didn't know you had it." A mad cackle burst from his lips causing Basil to scream again in the next room. Eva fought the urge to cover her ears as the piercing sound reverberated off the rocks.

Eva broke out into a sudden sweat that turned cold and set her shivering almost at once. "I…I think I should go now."

"The eagle, the lion, and the queen," Lord Vyr repeated breathless from his spell of laughter. "That's the key to stopping the iron storm and halting the breaking wind. Do you understand?"

She didn't have the slightest idea what the ancient lunatic was talking about, but Eva nodded anyway. "I've got it."

Lord Vyr seemed content. "Good, good! Now, off with you! I

must tend to Basil — he doesn't like being alone, no matter how prickly he pretends to be. Begone!"

"Thank you?" Eva wasn't quite sure what she was thanking him for.

But the old man wasn't listening. He gave her a dismissive wave and began whistling as he left her alone.

"I trust you know the way out, girl!" he shouted after her from the other chamber. "Good luck! And goodbye!"

As Lord Vyr's manic, howling laughter followed her down the passage, Eva wasn't sure if she felt better or worse after the encounter. Long after all sound faded, his words swirled in her head.

Prophecies, she reflected, were a much bigger pain in the rear than they were worth.

Chapter 8

Gryphons filled the skies — more than Eva had ever seen in the air at one time. They spread across the pale blue expanse above the Windswepts, perhaps the greatest mustering of Windsworn Rhylance had ever seen. Eva couldn't help but feel a surge of pride looking around at the riders and gryphons around her. Against any other force but the Smelterborn, they would have been unstoppable. Seeing the host in person, Eva allowed herself to think they just might have more than a chance to win the coming battle.

Fury soared through the air on the warm updrafts flapping his wings more to stretch than from a need to stay airborne. Although he'd been free to leave and hunt whenever he wished while Eva remained tethered in the city by her duties as princess, she knew Fury missed her company — he'd grown so surly and unruly in the past month that only Eva had been able to get near him without receiving an irritated hiss.

The blanket of new green grass and the bright spots of thousands of wildflowers gave way to stubborn drifts of snow and bare pale gray rock the higher into the Windswepts they flew. Below them, trails that would have normally been used by deer and elk returning the high country were bloated with siege equipment, horses, oxen, wagons, and soldiers. They cut through the beautiful spring scenery like a knife, reminding Eva that death for many loomed ahead during the season of rebirth.

They neared the Talon and the results of weeks of hard labor came into view. It was a marvel of construction, ingenuity, and cooperation between nations, but Eva still found the fortifications a blight on the mountain scenery. The pass itself was about a quarter mile wide and about three times as long, filled with nothing but slate rock. An earthen bulwark made from boulders, packed dirt and rows of timber stretched from one side to the other. Camps spilled out of the pass and down the western mountainside, filling the meadows and clearings with tents and muddy ground where troops drilled and made ready for the coming battle with the golems. Following the king on his blue-gray gryphon, Justicar, they dipped lower. Adelar and Andor's private wings followed, as well as Eva's newly-formed one — comprised of Sigrid, Wynn, Chel, Ivan and a couple other riders Eva had flown with in the past.

Eva wished she could have requested Tahl, but hadn't wanted to compromise his situation in the king's honor guard. Eva wasn't clueless enough to think that her uncles didn't know she and Tahl were more than friends but doubted either of them would approve of the engagement. Talented rider that he was, it didn't change the fact that Tahl was common birth and therefore, in the eyes of Adelar and Andor, unfit to marry her. She supposed that if it weren't for the war, they would have made her end the relationship.

Inside the pass, sheer rock rose up to impassable heights on either side. The snow-capped peaks far above were only accessible by flight and never free of their white crowns. As the mountain's walls loomed up on either side of them, shutting on the vibrant greens and other colors of the high country, Eva felt the mantle of war descend upon her. The only color came from the banners of the various regiments in the pass. Everything else seemed cold and lifeless — as muted as the Smelterborn's plate armor.

They flew over the first bulwark and then two more to reach the front lines. Here, the pass widened and descended into a steep slope down the eastern side of the mountain. Here on the eastern side, the earth had been churned into pure mud, on purpose Eva supposed, to make the steep climb even harder for the Smelterborn. Where the pass winged out on either side, Eva saw the Juarag's hide tents crowded against the cliffs, right where they had requested. Sabercats snarled and tussled with one another, fighting over the rotting carcasses of horses and oxen that had died from overwork and were tossed over the walls for the savage creatures to feed on. Rows of boulders lined the top of the pass, placed to roll down upon the Smelterborn when they began their ascent.

Gazing into the distance, she searched for any sign of the approaching army even though she knew they would be hidden below the timberline. The slope had been cleared of trees for almost a mile. Eva saw additional ditches, rows of fence and hastily built palisade walls. She tried not to imagine the slaughter that would take place there and didn't envy the soldiers sent out on those front lines with the Juarag. When retreat sounded, those soldiers would be faced with the same uphill climb through the mud as the Smelterborn. Rough-cut, wooden platforms interspersed on the slope held giant siege engines — catapults, ballistae and trebuchets ready to hurl even more rock down upon the Smelterborn. All well and good, until you realized nothing but a direct blow would stop the golems for good.

After a short loop around the eastern slopes, they wheeled back into the Talon and landed behind the second row of walls. A command tent had been set up in the one corner not occupied by soldiers, animals or supply wagons. Fury landed with a squelch in almost a foot of mud, hissing his displeasure. Eva frowned and slid out of the saddle into the mess, hoping she didn't lose a boot in the muck and make a fool of herself in front of the troops. Behind her, a growling curse announced Sigrid's landing. As soon as their riders were off, the gryphons leaped out of the muck to roosts on the craggy side of the pass. They hated the mud and wet almost as much as cats. Eva gave Fury a quick pat on the beak before the gryphon flew off to join his fellows, spraying flecks of mud over everyone in the process.

"Let it never be said that war isn't a glamorous thing," Andor muttered, flicking a speck of mud from his cheek and glaring after

Fury as he rose in the sky.

Eva stifled a laugh, which came out as a snort and a smirk. Shooting her an irritated glance to match the one he'd just given to Fury, Andor turned and headed for the tent. Eva groaned inwardly when she saw yet another map on the table, filled with even more wooden markers denoting the various military stations along the Windswepts. Their real-life counterparts stood at attention as Eva, the king, and lord commander took their places. General Brachus, an almost square man with a thick neck and beet red face, cleared his throat before pointing out various positions on the map with a riding crop.

"Our plan is to contain the Smelterborn to the eastern slope," the general said, mustache twitching as his eyes roved over the map. "We've dug four layers of ditches and embankments up the ridge. As needed, we fall back to the higher lines, all the while throwing rock down upon the Smelterborn with the siege engines. Sky bless us, the ironclads will never get past the first wall."

"And what if they do?" Eva asked. It was a good plan, but none of the men and women in the command tent had ever fought Smelterborn. "These aren't men — they feel nothing and care nothing for their losses, general. They will keep coming down to the last golem."

She could tell Brachus was fighting back a curt reply. Across the table, however, Andor and even Uthred nodded.

"We can fall back behind each wall as needed," the general said, making it perfectly clear he'd been about to mention this. "If worse comes to worse and we lose the pass entirely, the Scrawls will trigger a slide, shutting off the Talon completely."

Eva's eyes widened. The Talon was the main gateway to the eastern frontier — sure, with enough time and work, Scrawls and hundreds of laborers could remove the debris. Eva's concern was for the wounded soldiers that would be trapped along with the Smelterborn beneath tons of rock...

"But it won't get to that point, your highness," General Brachus said. It took Eva a moment to realize he was talking to her — she still hadn't gotten used to the new title and refused to let her friends speak to her with any formality. "We're confident we can hold the

Smelterborn on the eastern ridge. This battle will field the mightiest army ever assembled in modern history."

Eva thought this was probably true...if the general meant the golems.

"If we lose the pass, we will fall back to the capital," Andor said. "Gryfonesse will be evacuated and the people sent west to Pandion. That's why your role in the city is so important, Eva."

For being so confident in their initial battle strategy, the level of detail that had gone into the fall-back plans unsettled Eva. She knew it was wise to plan for every outcome but still felt a looming unease the war council did nothing to alleviate.

Eva spent the rest of the day touring the remaining defenses. She didn't believe it at first but Adelar informed her that the story of her journey east had spread and insisted she make an appearance before as many of the troops as possible.

"Everyone's talking about the princess who rides the red gryphon," the king said with a wry smile. "The Windsworn who fought a hundred Smelterborn and lived to tell the tale."

"What a bunch of nonsense," Eva scoffed. "I'm sure the tales get even more wild with each telling."

"Maybe so," Adelar said. "But seeing you gives them hope and that may be what it comes down to in the battle ahead, Eva."

She didn't have a response to that. Even so, Eva still felt like a storming idiot flying around the pass, offering weak smiles and awkward waves whenever soldiers and laborers paused to cheer and hail her.

At the end of the day, Eva was grateful to retire to her personal tent, although Adelar insisted on placing guards outside the door. The quarters were large enough for Sigrid, Chel, and Wynn to stay with her as well. Ivan rested in the Scrawls' camp, exhausted from his shift using rune magic to improve the fortifications in the pass. Eva had only caught glimpses of Tahl all day. She had a sneaking suspicion that Adelar and Andor made sure to keep her betrothed busy, especially when evening came.

"Wonder how long before the Smelterborn get here?" Wynn asked, mouth full of bread.

"You probably won't starve to death before then," Chel said, wrinkling her nose at the girl's atrocious manners. Sigrid took a similarly large bite of her own loaf and Eva shook her head at the pair.

"It's going to be a bloodbath," Eva said in a low voice. She wondered how many of those cheering soldiers had families waiting for them at home they would never see again.

"It is," Sigrid muttered, starting to sulk again. She'd been looking forward to the battle even though she'd seen firsthand what the Smelterborn were capable of. Tired of her friend's pouting, Eva gave Sigrid the choice to leave her guard and join the fight, but Sigrid only scoffed and shook her head.

"The last thing I want is to be responsible for the princess dying because I wasn't there to get you out of trouble."

"Lots of people are going to die here," Eva said. "And for what? We'll just delay the Smelterborn. As far as we know, there's plenty more out there, just waiting to strike again."

"Then we'll fight again when they come!" Sigrid said.

But Eva didn't think it was as simple as that. She thought of Seppo's broken memories and wondered if they would have been better off searching for the First Forge. Lord Vyr's words mingled among her thoughts as well. What in the sky did they mean?

Seppo and Soot were there in the camp, helping the other smiths. Eva had requested both of them in her guard and was surprised when Andor released the pair to return with her to the capital. She couldn't think of two people she'd rather have by her side and hoped their assignments in her wing would keep them out of harm's way.

Sigrid, Chel, and Wynn continued to talk but Eva withdrew herself from the conversation, choosing to thumb through a book she'd brought with her, the pages illuminated by the flickering lamplight bouncing off the tent walls. An hour or so later, the others settled down to sleep. Eva doused the light and felt waves of sleep washing over her when a shuffling sound outside the tent jolted her awake.

She listened, heart hammering as the sound drew closer. Her mind when to the Shadowstalkers and she leaned over the edge of her cot to grasp her sword, heart pounding. In the next moment, she realized no Smelterborn could walk that lightly, although this did little to relax her. Eva almost shouted for the guards when a familiar voice hissed through the canvas of the tent.

"Anybody awake in there?"

Eva let out the breath she'd been holding and slumped back on the cot. It was Tahl. Leaning over, she whispered through the tent wall. "What in the name of the sky are doing? If anyone finds out you're sneaking around camp to see me…"

"I'm off duty," Tahl whispered back through the curtain.

Eva looked around the tent and saw no one's breathing had changed. If anything Sigrid's snoring grew louder.

"Can you come out?" Tahl asked.

"You're crazy!" Eva glanced at the front of the tent. The guards made no sound or other indication that they suspected anything was up. In spite of her words, Eva slipped on her cloak. With some careful prying and lifting, she squeezed out beneath the back of the tent and into Tahl's arms.

"That's better," he said after they parted from a long kiss. "I'm afraid I can't stay long, though. I've got duty in four hours' time, and no matter where I am, they'll expect me to be back soon."

"I'm worried, Tahl," Eva said, resting against his chest. After spending the day as a figurehead for victory, it felt good to have someone else to lean on. "I don't think they're taking the Smelterborn serious enough."

Tahl kissed her forehead and Eva thought her legs might buckle. "Everything will be fine, you'll see. We've got a good position and basically the whole western half of Altaris to throw at them."

Eva didn't reply, trying to push aside her worries for the moment and savor their short time together. She knew that no matter the outcome of the battle, everything would be different. Being just Eva the Windsworn was a thing of the past. But here and now, she didn't have to pretend to be some heroine or symbol of hope.

"When are you going to tell your uncle about…" Tahl trailed off "You know, about us?"

Eva felt herself stiffen in his arms. "I…after the battle," she said. "I'm hoping things will settle down then and life can get back to normal, you know?"

"Whatever you think's best," he said, cupping her chin in his hand and smiling at her like Eva could do no wrong. This time, however, she felt more guilt than encouragement.

Still, Eva soaked in that cocky, self-sure smile, committing the moment to memory before pulling tight against him again. "Be careful out there, alright? If anything happens to my uncle, I'll never forgive you."

She looked up to show she was kidding. Tahl stepped back and spread his arms in mock indignation. "Oh and I'm just a meat shield for the Smelterborn?"

Before he could continue, Eva pulled him back and, for a long time, lost herself in his arms and lips. When they parted at last, heart racing and breath short, she knew she never wanted to have to say goodbye to him again. Tahl leaned in for another kiss. Summoning all of her resolve, Eva gave him a slight push away.

"Go on, hero," she said, smiling. "You need to get your beauty rest."

"Yeah, yeah, gotta look good for his highness," Tahl said, rolling his eyes. When he took a hesitant step back, Eva felt the space between them like a hammer blow.

"Take care of my future husband too," she said, winking.

Tahl grinned. "Of course, your grace."

Eva watched him stride off into the night and, for the thousandth time, wished more than anything she could go with him.

Chapter 9

Although the coming of the Smelterborn had been followed all the way by gryphon rider scouts, their actual arrival sent shockwaves through the Talon. Nervous mutters spread like a camp disease from one soldier to another until the entire army seemed to thrum with anxiety.

Eva negotiated with her uncles to allow her to observe the beginning of battle from afar, provided she left without question at their command. She agreed but didn't look forward to turning her back on the battle and returning to the city any more than Sigrid did.

While officers bellowed orders outside her tent, Eva shifted from foot to foot with nervous energy as she was fitted into her armor. It was beautiful work, the finest she'd ever seen Soot and Seppo craft, altered from her Windsworn battle gear to reflect her new status as the crown princess. Over shimmering chainmail, she wore dyed blue leathers trimmed with gold. A pair of golden wings were etched across the chest, matching the designs on her bracers. Still, she would have traded it for rags if it meant the Smelterborn would drop lifeless to the ground.

Around her, Sigrid and Wynn buckled on their Windsworn armor as well. Sigrid brimmed with cooped up frustration at being stuck in the rear away from the battle. Wynn, on the other hand, looked white as the snow-capped mountain peaks, reminding Eva she was just sixteen years of age, barely a full-fledged Windsworn.

Chel, eschewing armor aside from a chainmail vest, was busy painting herself with battle runes and war paint. As she streaked her face with the chalky paint, she hummed in her own language, an eerie, dirge-like sound that did nothing to help Eva's nerves.

"Relax," Soot said, placing a calming hand on Eva's shoulder as her attendant finished lacing up her leg bracers. The old smith looked almost like a different person to Eva — his thick leather apron and ember-burned shirt replaced with a dented breastplate and iron cap that covered his bald pate. Even so, she felt comforted by his presence. He gave Eva a reassuring wink and then placed her helm on her head. Like all of the Windsworn's helmets, two wings rose from either side and long guards covered her nose and cheeks. The burnished steel and silver glinted like a jewel in the sun — if nothing else, Eva at least dressed the part of the heroine.

In the distance, horns peeled, announcing the Smelterborn had cleared the tree line. Ivan ducked his head inside the tent. He had dark shadows under his eyes from days of labor preparing the defenses. Although not a citizen of Rhylance, Eva had specifically requested he join her guard. The Scrawl Elders were happy to comply.

"The show's about to begin."

Eva stepped off the stool she'd been on while being put in harness and buckled on her father's sword at her waist. Much like Soot's comforting hand, the dull gray blade filled her with courage as if her father was standing there beside her as well. She hoped she wouldn't have to draw it.

Pausing, Eva looked around at her closest friends. They'd been through storms, fights and overcome impossible odds together and she wouldn't have traded them for her own personal guard of golems — although Seppo was more than welcome. The golem stood outside the tent, waiting for them to emerge. Here and there, he recovered more bits and pieces of his memory, but nothing that really served them to defeat the Smelterborn. At first, the men viewed him with suspicion, but when they saw how much he could carry and work without getting tired, the golem was soon a welcome addition to the defenses.

As more horns pealed, Eva stepped outside the tent and blew out a long breath. Soldiers rushed to their posts as shouted orders echoed throughout the pass. Their gryphons stood saddled and waiting. Eva walked to Fury and a loud cheer went up from the surrounding soldiers.

Although she wanted to crawl back in her tent and hide, Eva smiled and raised a hand as she passed, face burning with embarrassment. When she reached Fury, the gryphon reared back on his hind legs and clawed at the air with his front talons. Throwing his head back, the red gryphon let loose a hair-raising scream.

"Show off," Eva muttered when he came back down.

"Remember," Soot cautioned as she swung onto the gryphon's back. "You gave your word. No joining the battle. You're to watch from a safe distance."

Eva nodded. "I know, I know."

Her foster father didn't look satisfied. "Promise me, Eva."

"I promise — no heroics today."

Since his journey with the eastern expedition years ago, Soot refused to fly. Eva guessed part of it was a fear of heights, although the blacksmith would never admit that. Seeing as how Seppo was too heavy to be borne by a gryphon, Soot reckoned he was just as good on the ground too, waiting in the rearguard. This last time was the dozenth he'd made Eva swear to stay clear of the fighting.

The rest of her guard mounted around Eva and Fury. Chel and Wynn on Wynn's tawny brindled gryphon, Lucia, and Sigrid and Ivan on Sven. Looking up, Eva saw gryphons streaming eastward. Eva and the rest rose in the air and flew straight down the pass, between the two peaks. More Windsworn ferried Scrawls onto the mountainsides, preparing to collapse sections of the pass if worse came to worse.

Although she knew she would be taking no part in the battle, Eva's stomach clenched in all-too-familiar twisted knots as they flew toward the battlefront. The shouts of men and women grew louder, accompanied by the deep thrum of siege machines flinging rocks and bolts at the golems.

They reached the first wall and found a small ledge with a high vantage point to land on. From their vantage, Eva surveyed most of the eastern ridge. Down the slope, just visible out of the tree line, the first wave of Smelterborn could be seen. They marched over fifty wide in a perfectly-spaced line. These were no scouts or stalkers, either, but full-sized fighting golems, a head taller than the biggest of men and almost twice as wide. Their dull gray armor seemed to soak up the sun, even the runes carved into their metal plates were muted, although Eva shuddered to think of the dark words inscribed there. Each bore a shield in one hand with either a mace, sword, or spear in the other — weapons so large a strong man like Soot would barely be able to lift them, let alone wield one in battle.

The Smelterborn continued to file from the trees. Eva's mouth went dry. She knew from the scouts how many there were, but seeing them in person, here at the Talon, seemed to increase their numbers tenfold.

Row upon row of golems marched toward the Talon, undeterred by the catapult shot, trebuchet fire and ballista bolts smashing all around them. Had they been a mortal army, the casualties would have been disastrous. A rock the size of a cow smashed into the ground in the third rank, scattering a handful of Smelterborn like rabbits. It kept rolling down through the golems until it passed out of sight in the midst of the gray army. Those not struck acted like they hadn't even seen it.

Eva guessed each projectile destroyed one or two golems at most — the direct hits that smashed in their helmets and torsos sent the familiar dark shadows arcing up through the sky and off into the pines. Eva was surprised to hear their terrible high-pitched screams even from their distance. Whatever demonic souls powered the Smelterborn broke free of their iron confines, fleeing to storm knew where. The rest of the golems struck by the projectiles merely clambered to their feet and fell back in line.

If nothing else, Eva saw how the boulders and gigantic bolts affected the Smelterborn's order. Large gaps appeared in the ranks. The golems all continued at the same pace, unable to move any faster to make up lost ground when bowled over by a shot. The sight offered little hope, however. Smelterborn still marched from the trees, their rearguard still out of sight.

The front lines reached the steeper part of the slope and Eva watched the leaders struggle in the slick mud. Several golems went down, flailing like overturned turtles until they righted themselves. Seeing their companions pass them by with no regard made them seem even more inhuman and dreadful to Eva, their sole purpose of genocide manifested.

Eva gripped Fury's lead lines tighter and tighter as the golems neared the first trenches.

The humans released volley after volley of arrows. Hundreds of shafts flew into the air, the majority clattering harmlessly off the Smelterborn's armor. Interspersed, she saw gusts of wind, balls of flame and streaks of ice from the few Scrawls mixed in with the regular soldiers working their rune kennings.

After what seemed both an eternity and a moment, the Smelterborn, splattered with mud, their ranks split like a gap-toothed old man, reached the first ditch. They set about hacking at the palisade walls and sharpened stakes as calm as a man chopping firewood. In short order, they were through.

Slaughter followed. For a few minutes, the soldiers, lightly equipped so that they would be able to fall back without the encumbrance of plate armor, were mowed down like ripe wheat. It didn't take long for the soldiers to break, throwing down their weapons to scramble uphill on all fours like terrified animals. Eva felt herself growing sick but forced herself not to look away — the least she could do for the fallen.

The Smelterborn went about their bloody work in complete silence, their first attack punctuated only by the screams of terrified men and women. In a few horrific minutes, only the dead and the dying remained at the first trench. When the last of the living scrambled past them, caked in mud, the second trench began raining arrows while the siege machines continued to pound away at the deeper lines.

Through it all, Smelterborn continued marching out of the trees. Eva bit her lip. If they couldn't hold the golems here, what chance did she have?

Chapter 10

Afternoon passed into evening. The Smelterborn continued climbing the slope. Their progress slowed as the ridge steepened near the entrance of the pass, but nothing could stop the iron golems. Nothing gave them pause or reason to retreat — not that they comprehended retreat. Had the defenders been facing a human army, it would have already been soundly defeated, a credit to the bravery of the soldiers fighting and the design of the defenses and fortifications. But the Smelterborn were not men and cared nothing for the odds they faced or their comrades who perished.

Eva and Fury grew restless on their ledge, watching the battle unfold below. The group as a whole said little, the tension palpable between them. Whenever a soldier fell, Eva's hatred for the Smelterborn grew and she wished for nothing more than to destroy them down to the last golem.

Soon the front ranks of the Smelterborn were inside the range of the siege weapons. Even so, the brave engineers continued to fire on the rear part of the army, refusing to abandon their posts as the Smelterborn drew closer and closer, inching up the hill like a giant gray snail, slowly but surely.

The majority of the defenders fell back over the walls as the golems crossed the last ditch. They swarmed up ladders and ropes and crowded through a single gate, burdened with the wounded and more than a few dead.

Up above on the ledges, the Scrawls worked in small groups to channel their powers together, creating ice and firestorms. They hurled boulders through the air down onto the Smelterborn, although this did little more than the siege projectiles or arrows. Rune magic worked effectively to stop to the golems one-on-one, but in large groups, the attacks only slowed the Smelterborn's progress.

Overhead, gryphon riders dived at the Smelterborn, dropping rocks and logs on their heads as they passed by. When the first wing made its pass, one bold rider urged his gryphon closer, attempting to snag a Shadowstalker golem and pull them into the air. Instead, rider and gryphon crashed into the mass of dull gray iron. Eva squeezed her eyes shut at the sounds of dying gryphon, screaming and shrieking as the golems chopped them to pieces.

As terrible as it was to see a fellow rider and his gryphon go down, Eva couldn't believe the heavy toll the Juarag and their sabercats paid. As soon as the golems reached the second trench, the Juarag had charged, smashing into the side of the Smelterborn with more force than Eva expected. She'd seen war cats in action one on one, but together, they struck like a giant hammer. The sheer power, and ferocity, of the beasts could bowl over even the heaviest Smelterborn.

They died in waves, but their crazed sacrifice slowed the golems' progress and the nimble sabercats could move across the muddy slope almost as fast as a gryphon flying overhead. Although she'd spent the better part of two years protecting the eastern borders of Rhylance against the same marauding raiders and their fearsome mounts, Eva's heart broke each time a sabercat's bawling death scream ripped through the air. The corpses of the fearsome beasts dotted the ridge and Eva found something tragic and sad in their still, dead forms.

Eva's hands tingled and she realized she'd been clutching the front of Fury's saddle in a death grip. She forced them loose and drew out a long breath, feeling her chest relax as if there'd been a gryphon sitting on it. The sun waned in the sky and Eva realized they'd been sitting there watching for hours. Although she felt sick, she forced herself to drink deep from the lukewarm water in her canteen and force down a few strips of meat and dried fruit from one of her saddlebags. Smelling the food, Fury twisted his head around to give her a guilt-laden look. The gryphons had all been released the night before to find game and she knew he wasn't starving but Eva tossed a piece of dried meat in the air for Fury anyway.

By now, perhaps a tenth of the Smelterborn lay defeated on the ridge. Eva guessed for each empty suit of armor, at least three human soldiers had lost their lives with twice as many wounded. After the second palisade fell, the defenders fell back and only attacked with arrows and siege machines, realizing close combat amounted to nothing more than slaughter.

The Smelterborn inched up the hill as sure as the setting sun, within bowshot of the first wall now. Down below, Eva saw Adelar dressed in gold-chased armor, shouting words of encouragement and waving his spear from atop the first wall. She'd spotted Andor off and on throughout the day flying about and directing orders.

Eva ground her teeth, frustrated at being stuck doing nothing, watching the battle unfold. By now, they'd all dismounted and were sitting on the edge of the ledge, solemn and quiet. Eva knew everyone else was thinking the same thing as her. As they watched, her hands drummed on the hilt of her sword and she couldn't help but think what even a hundred such blades could do. When she'd returned home with it, Soot and Seppo had studied her father's sword, but even after Seppo's memory began to return and he recognized the construction, he'd regretfully told them he couldn't replicate it. Eva offered it to both of her uncles before the battle began, but Adelar and Andor insisted she keep it with her. Tahl had told her the same thing the night before.

She knew her father wouldn't have stood for waiting around like they were. Aleron and his golden gryphon, Sunflash, would have been right in the middle of the fray, striking Smelterborn down left and right. But that was the difference between them, Eva supposed. In his younger years, Aleron had earned the name "the Pride of Rhylance" for his heroics, while Eva did as she was told, sitting on the rock, stomach churning, anxiety pressing upon her far heavier than her armor did, which was saying something.

She reached for the Wonder around her neck and clutched it tight. Although she couldn't see the blue, yellow and rose-colored lights twinkling from its stone, Eva felt reassured by its presence. For not the first time, she wished there was a way to use it against the Smelterborn as a whole. But if the Ancients had ever devised ways to fight the golems en mass instead of with stones and swords, no one had uncovered it.

The day passed in a long, slow drag of anxiety, boredom, and frustration for all of the companions sitting on the ledge. The gryphons grew tired and restless but were forced to stay grounded in the event they had to make a quick escape. It was even greater torture for them — the sights and smells of the battle below set them on edge in a way only open skies could relieve.

Sigrid heaved out a long sigh and punched the rock beside her. "I hate this," she said, teeth grinding together. Around her, Wynn, Chel, and Ivan nodded in agreement without taking their eyes off the battle below.

"We should *do* something," Ivan said, fingers and lips twitching as he imagined the kennings he'd chant to hurl destruction down on the Smelterborn below.

Over and over, the thought kept running through Eva's mind that they could slip into the fray, probably unnoticed. She'd even volunteered to pass messages — anything was better than sitting there doing nothing. She'd started to think waiting at the citadel in Gryfonesse wouldn't be so bad. At least there, she wouldn't have to experience the battle firsthand.

As if sensing their restlessness, a dark, earthy brown gryphon winged toward them and landed on the ledge. Its rider, a fair-haired man near their age named Vallon, smacked his fist against his chest and bowed before Eva.

"Your Highness —" he began.

"Oh, storm off, Vallon," Sigrid said, standing up. She'd been waiting for someone to take out her ire on and the poor messenger proved to be the perfect target. "You can call her Eva, just like the rest of us."

Vallon gave a nervous cough, eyes darting away from Sigrid. She was known for her nasty temper throughout the Gyr and it wouldn't have been out of character for her to pummel him right then and there, especially in her current foul mood.

"My — Eva, uh, the lord commander and king have requested that you return to your tent and prepare to return to Gryfonesse at first light."

"What! You go back and tell my uncle —"

"Eva!"

Before she could finish, Andor wheeled toward them on the back of his pale gray gryphon, Stormwind. "Get out of here!" he shouted without landing. "That's an order!"

Without waiting for a reply, Andor and Stormwind shot off again, joining with another wing as they soared down over the Smelterborn, dropping debris on their helmeted heads. Fuming, Eva clenched her teeth and swung up onto Fury's saddle with enough force that the gryphon squawked and staggered to keep his balance.

Vallon shrugged as if to remind them he was just the messenger then launched off the cliff ledge before any of them could take out their frustration on him. Scowling so hard her face hurt, Eva whistled and Fury launched into the air, headed west.

Halfway through the Talon, Eva turned, wondering if they could sneak away in the twilight. But her uncles were one step ahead of her. Three riders trailed her group, no doubt to make sure they did as they were told. Eva vented a sigh and was half-tempted to try to lose them in the dark. Instead, she pointed Fury down to an open space near their tent. As soon as they touched down, Soot was at her side.

"What's going on? We've been getting reports from the front but it's been all hearsay. Someone said the Smelterborn breached the first wall and then someone else said they hadn't even made it up the ridge yet."

Eva related the battle as they'd seen from their vantage point and felt disheartened by Soot's worried expression when she finished. His face confirmed that things were going as bad as she'd thought.

"Only half a day and they're already almost to the pass…"

Shadows from the spluttering torches flickered off the rocks. The wind seemed to blow without end through the Talon, a cold bitter chinook birthed on the western sea that grew more violent and icy the farther east it went. Up in the mountains, winter still refused to give away to spring.

"We're doing all we can," Eva said, trying to fight the darkening mood settling over them. "The lines can only hold for so long against them."

"Might not be long enough," Soot muttered.

Suddenly tired from a day sitting around in armor, Eva began unbuckling her harness. The weight of it had dragged at her through the day, almost driving her insane, and she wanted nothing more than to shrug it off and go to bed. She reasoned the best thing she could do right now was save her strength for when it was needed. On one hand, she wanted to do her share to defend her country and people. On the other, she knew things would be dire indeed if she and her guard were required to fight.

Soot told them he and Seppo would keep watch — they'd spent the entire day in the forge and Eva realized their assignment had probably been even more boring than hers, although much more intensive. She convinced Soot to leave Seppo alone outside the tent with instructions to wake them if anything changed. Although he tried to resist at first, the dark circles under Soot's eyes revealed his exhaustion and he did little more than grumble at the suggestion to get some sleep with the rest of them.

Wynn helped Eva out of her armor and, as the cumbersome mail fell away, Eva felt better at once. Having spent the whole day in each other's company, nagging and needling at one another, the friends passed around some muttered, curt goodnights and everyone drifted off to silence or sleep if they were lucky.

In spite of her worries, Eva slipped into a deep slumber almost as soon as they blew out the lanterns. Sometime in the night, she dreamed she was at the mouth of the pass again. This time, however, it was almost impossible to see, the sky starless overhead.

Eva gasped as she realized she was the only one standing in the midst of hundreds of mangled, dead soldiers and dozens of defeated Smelterborn. She felt an overwhelming urge to get help, to make sure none of the Smelterborn had made it through the pass, but no matter how much she yelled, no one answered. She realized no one was alive to answer.

Seized by panic, Eva ran west through the pass, stumbling over hacked and mutilated corpses, sobbing at the sight of familiar faces grimacing in frozen expressions of death. On the verge of hysteria, she reached inside her tunic for her Wonder. When she pulled the necklace out, however, the white stone refused to shine.

She reached the end of the pass and stopped, looking down to see Gryfonesse below her, its white stones illuminated by a hundred fires roaring in the night sky. Eva's mouth went dry and she looked to the right of the city and saw the Gyr. Gryphons wheeled around its peak, highlighted by the fires in the capital below. Staring, she realized their bodies were halfway rotted, the firelight reflecting through the holes in their bodies and wings. The riders on their backs cackled and screamed, more skeleton than human.

Look upon your doom.

The voice came from all around and inside her head as well. Eva turned and a pitch black Smelterborn with blazing red eyes stood behind her, a great horned helm on its head, enormous smithing hammer hanging from its hand. The runes blazing across its armor burned with the flames of a thousand forges.

I will burn the impurities from this land until nothing remains!

A great rumbling rippled through the ground and Eva fell to her knees as a howling wind screeched down the pass, knocking the gryphons out of the sky into the inferno of the blazing city below. Their dying screams, mixed with the howls of humans and the piercing cries of sabercats, filled Eva's ears and mind. She clasped her hands to her head and pinched her eyes shut, but could not escape the awful noise.

Eva collapsed and thrashed on the ground, wishing anything — even her own death — would make the sound stop. She rolled over and saw the black-armored Smelterborn standing above her. She grappled for her Wonder and thrust in front of her like a shield, but the chain and stone crumbled to dust in her hands. Laughing, the golem hefted its mighty hammer overhead. Eva curled in a ball, prepared to be crushed and —

"Wake up!"

Yanked from her dream, Eva jerked upright. Her breath came in ragged gasps and sweat drenched her shirt and hair. Eyes wide with fright, she looked around the tent and found everyone staring at her.

"What in the sky were you dreaming of?" Sigrid asked. "We thought you were going to break something the way you were thrashing around!"

Wynn stared, eyes almost as wide as Eva's and Chel made the sign against evil. Approaching Eva like he might a sabercat, Ivan held out his hand and muttered a kenning. Green light floated from his hand and enveloped Eva in its soothing glow. Eva took a deep breath and relaxed. She reached for her Wonder and was reassured at the warmth pulsing from the stone.

Between Ivan's rune magic and the Wonder, she felt better at once. Even so, the memory of the midnight golem with the blazing red eyes loomed in her mind.

"It spoke to me," she said in a faint, cracked voice. Tears ran down her face.

"What did?" Soot asked. He knelt beside her and placed his callused hands over hers. Eva reflected later that she'd never seen him so concerned. "Eva, what did you dream?"

Unable to speak, Eva glanced at Ivan. Their eyes met and she saw the same terror in his eyes. He gave the smallest nod and she knew he'd seen the same thing in his visions. The Scrawl swallowed hard and his face drained of color.

"*It's coming,*" Ivan whispered.

Horns blasted in the distance and a big iron arm reached inside the tent, followed by Seppo's round head. "Hello," he said, in the same voice he might wish them a good morning. "Please pardon my intrusion, but I believe something bad is happening at the wall."

67

Chapter 11

After another kenning from Ivan, Eva was able to stand and made her way outside with the rest. Soldiers rushed by them, running to the east. Soot grabbed a passing soldier, nearly yanking him over as he wheeled him around to face them. "What's going on?"

"The Smelterborn have broken through the eastern wall, sir," the man said in a hurried voice. "King Adelar and Lord Commander Andor have called for reinforcements as the men try to pull back to safety behind the fortifications in the middle of the pass. My commander was ordered to commit our reserve at once. The Scrawl, Maizoro, and Pandion companies are doing the same."

Before the man could finish, Eva ran into her tent and began dressing as fast as she could. Wynn followed in behind her and together they pulled the mail over her and buckled on the rest of the armor as fast as they could. Although it was only a few minutes later, to Eva it felt like hours before they were all dressed in their gear. Outside, the gryphons shifted nervously in the mounting chaos, eager to be off the ground. As Eva strode back out of the tent, Soot and Seppo stepped in front of her.

"Where are you off to, missy?" Soot asked, folding his arms on his chest.

Eva frowned. "I'm going to help," she said. "They'll need everyone they can get."

Soot shook his head. "Not a stormin' chance. You get back to the city, Eva. Adelar and Andor need you there."

"I can help here," Eva said, trying to control her mounting temper. "No one else —"

Another series of horns sounded, followed by distant shouts and screams echoing down the Talon.

"Something is wrong," Soot said, face growing even more grave.

They rushed forward up the earthen rampart until they stood atop the wall. In the faint torchlight, it was hard to see much farther down the pass. Now and then, a blast of fire streaked across the sky or shot down from the sides of the pass, briefly illuminating companies of soldiers rushing east. Eva shuddered, the scene conjuring memories of her nightmare. She guessed it was still a few hours before sunrise, although not even a faint glimmer of light showed in the eastern sky. A pale sliver of moon provided scant light. They couldn't have been asleep for more than a couple of hours — what could have gone so wrong?

"We should get back," Soot said, reaching for Eva.

She shrugged his grip away. "I'm not running anymore. Let's get the others and see what's going on — that's the only way we're going to find anything out."

Soot frowned, the wrinkle on his bald head spreading like cracked earth. "Eva you know —"

"If there's something we can do to help, we have to try," she said, cutting him off.

Wading back through the soldiers rushing eastward, Eva and Soot found the rest of her guard awaiting their return by the tent.

"Well?" Sigrid asked, arms folded. "What's going on?"

Eva shook her head. "Can't tell but we're going to look. Everyone in?"

Sigrid pumped her fist in the air, eyes shining with the familiar glint she got every time the prospect of battle drew near. Ivan grinned and cracked his knuckles, shaking out his fingers in preparation for working magic. Chel gave a solemn nod and Wynn tried to put on a brave face, but Eva could see the trepidation in the girl.

"Anyone who wants to wait here with the gryphons can." Eva looked away from Wynn so it didn't appear she was talking just to the younger girl. Although she was technically Windsworn now, Eva knew Wynn had never been in a real battle before. Then again, neither had Eva, at least not one of the size they fought now. She looked at each of them in turn but no one wanted to stay behind.

Satisfied, Eva walked over to Fury and the other gryphons, knowing they were as restless as the humans to join the fray. But in the darkness, the chances of them being wounded or killed weren't worth the risk.

"You've got to stay here," she told Fury, taking a step back as the gryphon tossed his head and hissed. "I know, I know, you don't like it either, but they'll be plenty of fighting to go around. Now promise?"

Fury reluctantly dipped his head. Eva wasn't sure she could trust him to stay but had no more time to press the issue. Returning to the tent, her body groaned as the weight of her armor returned. Fully armed, Eva faced them again.

"Let's go."

With Eva, Soot and Seppo in the lead, they picked their way through the chaotic mass of men and women heading for battle. Passing over the ladder of the rear wall — Seppo merely jumped over, landing hard enough to shake the ground — they made it halfway to the second wall before meeting the wounded soldiers in retreat. Eva grimaced at the gruesome injuries on the living as well as the mangled dead. The expressions of the men and women they passed ranged from terrified to dull blankness, the latter the most unnerving.

Each step she took, Eva grew sicker and sicker as her surroundings became more like those of her dream. She reached a trembling hand up, put it down the front of her mail and wrapped her fingers around her mother's Wonder. Unlike her nightmare, however, the stone shone with its familiar, reassuring light, giving Eva new resolve.

Within a quarter mile of the second wall, the cacophony rose even louder. The screams of the dying, officers bellowing and clangor of arms and armor resounded throughout the canyon cutting through the dark night.

A fresh batch of retreating soldiers rushed by as fast as they could, burdened with the wounded. Soot grabbed one soldier on the shoulder who limped by, using a spear as a crutch. "What's going on up there?"

"They — they took the western wall!" the man shouted. "We were holding but then this — this thing came! A golem three times the size of the others! Smashed through our soldiers like they weren't even there! They said the lord commander and his gryphon went down fighting it. I didn't —"

"Eva, wait!"

Eva ignored Soot's call and ran as fast as she could, pushing through the soldiers. Thumping footsteps told her Seppo followed at her heels, but Eva didn't glance back to see if the others were keeping up. Nothing mattered but finding her family.

Even aided by frenzied panic, Eva soon slowed, lungs and legs burning from the weight of her chain mail, sweat running down her back, soaking her padded tunic beneath the armor. Dropping her hands to her knees, she sucked in a couple of deep breaths. Before she could stand up, Seppo swept her off of her feet as if she weighed no more than a baby.

"I've got you, mistress Eva!" His voice lacked the slightest hint of exhaustion, and he hadn't even broken his stride to pick her up.

Eva started to protest, then realized hitching a ride with Seppo was probably the fastest way to the front lines. She glanced back to see the rest of her guard trying to keep up. Looking ahead, she saw men and women surging to the top of the wall, before being thrown back just as quickly by advancing Smelterborn. In the thick of the battle, she spotted Adelar and Andor both still standing. The pair fought back to back, their gryphons swooping down at the golems from overhead.

Seppo waded through the soldiers, a couple swinging at him until they saw his blue eyes and realized he wasn't attacking them. Even so, Eva insisted he put her down at the bottom of the earthen mound, the errant swings a little too close for comfort. On her own feet, she climbed the mound, pressing through the knot of soldiers to reach her uncles.

"We need more spears to the left!" she heard Andor shout. "Where are the reinforcements from Maizoro?"

"Stay strong, men and women of Rhylance!" Adelar added. "We can hold! *We must hold!*" He turned toward Eva just as she reached the top of the bulwark, eyes widening in surprise.

"Eva! What are doing? *Get out of here!*"

"We came to help!" Eva looked over the rampart and saw masses of Smelterborn just a stone's throw away, jammed in tight, shields up, pushing forward.

"You've got to get out of here!" This time it was Andor yelling. He waved a hand, signaling one of his wing to come and no doubt escort Eva back to the rear. Seeing Tahl approaching, Eva almost collapsed in relief. It took everything she had not to rush forward and throw her arms around him."

"No!" Eva shouted again as the rest of her guard reached her side. Both Andor and Adelar gave Soot a dirty look as if to say they had expected better of him, but the smith was doubled over, huffing and puffing and didn't notice.

"What happened?" Eva asked. "We couldn't get a clear story from anyone."

"We held the front wall for most of the evening and into the night," Andor said, shouting to be heard over the battle. "But then this enormous golem came out of the trees. We've never seen it before. It cut through our defenses like they weren't even there. We've been pulling back ever since — our weapons can barely slow it down, let alone damage it."

Eva looked out over the mass of Smelterborn pushing against the wall and for a brief moment thought of all the dead and dying trampled beneath their iron boots.

"We can't hold much longer," Adelar said, pulling her close to talk in her ear. "You must return to Gryfonesse and prepare the city's defenses."

"I don't —"

Before Eva could finish, shouts of alarm rose to their left.

Smelterborn surged over a gap in the defenses, cutting a wide circle on top of the wall as more climbed up behind them.

"Go!" Andor yelled. "Tahl, get her out of here!"

Tahl grabbed Eva's elbow. She jerked away and drew her sword to enter the fray but before she could take a step, the pass reverberated with a deafening thunderclap.

BOOM

Everyone — men, women, and Smelterborn — halted. The ground shuddered beneath Eva's boots.

BOOM

Eva look to the sky, expecting to see lightning flashing above. The thunder reverberated through the pass and Eva wondered if the Scrawls had decided to collapse the mountain on top of them.

BOOM

All eyes turned toward the eastern end of the pass. Barely visible in the darkness, a monstrous shadow approached towering over the other golems as if they were children.

BOOM

Rooted to the spot, Eva stared in horror at the colossal Smelterborn lurching toward the wall.

Chapter 12

The regular-sized Smelterborn parted before the colossus, lining a wide path down the middle of the Talon. When the enormous golem passed, the others filled in behind it, marching as fast as they could to keep up with its lengthy strides. Horror flooded Eva as she saw its armor, black as the night surrounding it, and deep red eyes burning with the ferocity of a thousand chunks of molten iron. With every step, the colossus beat a mace the size of a tree against a shield as big as a wagon, the cause of the thunderous booms.

"*Run*, Eva. RUN!" Andor shoved her away, but Adelar grabbed Eva's hand and held it tight.

"Promise me, Eva," he said, blue eyes piercing through her. "Promise me you'll hold the city."

Overcome with shock, Eva only nodded. The colossal golem drew closer, arrows and spears falling from its armor like straw thrown at an anvil.

"Eva, come on!"

Tahl's worried face drew Eva to her senses. She drew her sword, scooting sideways down the earthen slope as the rest of her guard filled in around her. The Smelterborn resumed fighting and flanked the soldiers on the wall. In such close quarters, and without the aid of numbers on their side, the human warriors fell left and right, their weapons all but useless against the golems.

A man in front of her went down, leg buckling from a Smelterborn's sweeping blow. As the golem raised its club overhead, Eva leaped forward to parry the killing strike. It took all of her strength to swing her sword hard enough to knock the blow aside and she stumbled forward, tripping on the injured man beneath her. The Smelterborn recovered faster than any human could have and Eva just managed to side step another swing.

Two more Smelterborn hemmed in around the first and Eva shouted at the man to crawl away. The golems stomped toward her and Eva knew she had no hope of fighting three at once. Suddenly Tahl, Soot, Seppo and the rest were at her side. The Smelterborn stared at Seppo for a long moment as if in faint recognition. It only lasted a moment. The enemy golems shook their heads and advanced.

Eva yelled and ducked beneath the swing of the original Smelterborn, this time thrusting her sword up and into its chest. The runes on her blade glowed like the weapon had just been drawn from the forge, passing through the thick metal plate like paper. Wrenching the blade free, Eva just managed to stumble out of the way as the golem crashed to the ground.

An awful roar shattered the air — an ear-splitting mixture of grating metal and hammer blows. Seppo slammed into the Smelterborn to Eva's left, still bellowing. The rest of her guard attacked the one on the right. The two golems crashed together like a pair of bulls, the Smelterborn abandoning its sword and shield to grapple hand to iron hand with Seppo. For a moment, they struggled back and forth, arms locked. But whatever craftsmanship had gone into Seppo's making proved to be superior. Surging forward, the golem threw the Smelterborn down and locked its hands around its opponent's helmet. In one mighty wrench, Seppo tore his opponent's head from its shoulders before the Smelterborn could recover.

Eva gaped. She'd never seen Seppo hurt so much as a fly in almost two decades living with him. Now he charged forward like a terrible war machine, shouldering aside another golem in a terrifying display of raw strength. Eva might have remained rooted to the spot if not for

Wynn tugging at her arm.

"C'mon!"

Wynn yanked Eva down the Talon as Ivan threw a blast of ice into the face of the other Smelterborn and the rest of her guard fell in around her. Glancing over her shoulder Eva saw Seppo take on two enemy golems at once, caving one's helmet in with a fearsome punch before hurtling the other back into its counterparts behind.

Soot shouted for Seppo to join them as reinforcements surged around them to stem the iron tide of Smelterborn marching through the breach in the wall. Eva's guard pressed in around her, fighting to keep from being borne back toward the front lines.

"Make way for the princess!"

"*Make way for the princess!*"

Eva saw the wall swarming with Smelterborn now, their colossal champion reaching down to tear out chunks of earth and rock and cast them upon the human soldiers like a two-armed catapult. Neither of her uncles could be seen. Eva's stomach rolled, imagining the worst.

"No time to stop now, missy," Soot said, putting an arm around Eva's shoulder to pull her along. "Keep moving!"

They found enough room to jog, still dodging oncoming reinforcements. Farther back, most were in ordered lines and columns, having yet to succumb to the chaos at the front of the fight.

Back at the third wall, officers stood on top of the earthen mound, waving their swords and directing their regiments forward. Scores of Pandion spearmen marched in unison, equipped in heavy plate. More Scrawl rune masters ran forward in small groups, the tattoos on their exposed skin glowing as they prepared their kennings and supplicated to the Muse Mother. Row upon row of Sorondaran knights, most of the reserve, shouldered their war hammers, thronged by Mairozon bowmen and lancers who had abandoned their horses. Roused from sleep, dozens of gryphon riders sped overhead down the pass toward the battle.

Several dark shapes pulled up and fluttered down above them, their screams revealing them as gryphons. Eva recognized Fury and ran to his side. She knew at once something must be wrong if he'd left the tent.

Eva swung onto his back and pulled Chel up behind her. Muttering curses, Soot climbed on Lucia while the others all mounted around him, leaving only Seppo on the ground. Eva saw Soot's look of trepidation and knew only the dire circumstance got the smith to climb onto the back of a gryphon and break his vow of never flying again.

As soon as they were airborne, Eva's feelings of something wrong were confirmed. Off to the west, she spotted soldiers running to the north, small dark shapes illuminated by flickering torches. Horses screamed and broke free, bolting down the slope into the trees. A burst of Scrawl fire lit up the cliffs a short distance from Eva's tent and she saw Smelterborn Shadowstalkers and scouts leaping down from the rocks.

"We're being flanked!" Eva shouted to the others. Without a command, Fury shifted his flight leading them toward the attack.

Eva glanced back and saw the others flying in close succession behind her. Down below, Seppo hurtled past human soldiers racing toward the rear.

Nearing the golems, Eva and Chel leaped from the gryphon's back and Fury hurtled himself at the Smelterborn, catching one in the face with his talons and bowling it over. Ignoring her dry mouth and the empty, hollow, nervous feeling inside of her, Eva ran toward the rocks and drew her father's rune sword.

Instinct took over and Eva slashed through a Shadowstalker pinning a man to the ground with its spear. The sword sliced through the thinner, lighter armored golem like an ax taken to a sapling tree. The leaner golem split in half, wailing as the spirit trapped within fled into the night. Without checking the man on the ground, Eva charged a scout about to cast a spear at the incoming gryphons and took its arm off at the elbow joint.

Swinging his massive two-handed sword like a club, Soot struck one of the Shadowstalkers in the head, not killing it but knocking it to the ground. Sigrid screamed, sounding more gryphon than woman and cast one of her axes, catching a Smelterborn scout just right in the helmet. It collapsed lifeless to the ground. Tahl, Chel, and Wynn rushed to protect Eva's back while Ivan spouted words faster than Eva thought imaginable, fire and ice shooting from his hands.

The rearguard rallied around them. Together they drove the Smelterborn back against the cliffs but more of the golems leaped down from above. No matter how many Eva cut down with her blade, Ivan with his rune magic or the others through brute force, another always sprang into its place. Even Seppo did little to discourage them, ripping heads and limbs from their armored torsos like they were scarecrows.

In a brief lapse in the battle, Eva watched awestruck as the golem worked his destruction. Seeing Seppo in the midst of battle made the other Smelterborn, even the leaner, agile Shadowstalkers, look like children's toys next to his precision and skill. Eva would have given almost anything for a hundred more just like him.

The last Smelterborn fell and a ragged cheer rose from the survivors. Many defenders lay dead around them, at least three for every fallen Smelterborn. It was a terrible price but not as heavy as the one paid by the defenders in the pass. By the time the last Smelterborn fell, Eva and the rest were exhausted, shoulders slumped, weapons dangling, chests heaving. Only Seppo looked unaffected, humming as he piled the broken bits of Smelterborn together.

"We need to get to Gryfonesse," Tahl said as soon as they'd caught their breath and taken a sip of water. "The Talon won't hold much longer."

Eva gave a tired nod. They walked toward the gryphons and were about to take flight when a flash of gray passed. Stormwind landed before them, a weary Andor sliding from the saddle. Eva ran toward her uncle with new hope, grateful to find him alive and sure the lord commander's presence meant the tide had turned.

When Andor looked at her, Eva's leaping heart plummeted in her chest. Andor's piercing blue eyes were dull and swollen. In the faint light, he looked gray and ragged, aged beyond his years in the short time since she'd last seen him.

"What is it?" Eva asked, grasping her uncle's arms. "What

happened?"

The lord commander bowed his head and sank to one knee.

"The king is dead," he said in a broken, rasping voice. "Long live Queen Evelyn."

Chapter 13

As everyone around her sank to her knees, cold dread settled over Eva. Dumbfounded, she stared at Andor's bowed head — her last living blood kin.

"We tried to retreat to the middle wall," the lord commander said in a flat voice. "But by the sky, there was nothing we could do against the colossus. It swept aside twenty men with every blow of its mace. Adelar... he commanded me to oversee the retreat and said he was falling back here. Instead, he and Justicar went straight for that sky-cursed monster. By the time I saw...it was too late. They flew right at its head, I don't think the golem expected that. By the tempest, his lance struck true, right in its eye...but...there was just no way they could get away in time. The colossus fell and they went down beneath it...took a score or more of Smelterborn with it, crushed them all beneath its weight. I wanted...I wished I could have..."

Andor trailed off, tears running down his grief-lined face. Eva sank down next to him, and they clutched one another, overcome in grief. She couldn't believe it. She'd just seen Adelar, just spoken with him. The wounds of her father's death tore open once more, threatening to overcome her.

Wiping his eyes, the lord commander let out a long, ragged breath and rose, lifting Eva with him. She swayed, leaning against her last uncle for support, unable to stand on her own.

"I've ordered everyone to fall back to the city and the Gyr," Andor said. "And sent word ahead to have the Juarag refugees moved north immediately. We must go. Once I see you safe to the city, I will return and oversee the withdrawal."

Eva managed to nod, still stricken with grief, unable to grasp anything with her numb mind. Andor walked back to Stormwind and Eva turned, in a daze. The others rose, watching her uncertainly. It was Tahl who came forward first, hesitant as if looking at a different person other than his beloved.

"Just get back to the city, that's all you've got to do right now," he said. "We'll figure the rest out then, okay?" He squeezed her on the shoulder, those confident, reassuring eyes pulling her from the fog.

Nodding to the others, she ran a hand along Fury's neck and stepped around his lowered wing into the saddle. Chel followed in silence. In the air, the stillness grew between them. Eva tried to silence the rush of thoughts overwhelming her. She wasn't ready to run a kingdom, not by a long shot. Just like she'd told Adelar, she was supposed to have years to learn and watch. She scoffed at herself. So much for that.

"What will we do now?" Chel asked.

"I …" Eva let out a long deep sigh. "I have no idea."

Chel gave Eva a gentle squeeze and continued the embrace as they flew. "I will help you. You are my sister, remember."

Eva nodded, throat tight. She struggled to fight the tears. One of the last things Aleron had said to her and Chel, before he'd sacrificed himself, was that Eva and Chel had to look after one another. Andor wasn't her last living family after all, but then again, neither was Chel. She knew she could — and would — rely on Soot, Sigrid, Wynn, Ivan, and Tahl.

They flew well into morning before Andor touched down in a small mountain clearing surrounded by tall, dark, brooding pines. Eva knew he would have liked to make it all the way back to the city, but the gryphons were as exhausted as their riders, heads and tails drooping.

Eva hadn't considered the grief the creatures must have felt. For every rider that died, a gryphon perished as well. Although the creatures were hatched from hundreds of different broods, they still formed a large family, just like the Windsworn. The massive loss of the majestic animals was a tragedy in and of itself.

She pulled out her necklace, clenching the Wonder stone in her hand, trying to absorb some of its light into her shadowed heart. They would rebuild, she vowed in silence. They would destroy the Smelterborn.

"We cannot rest for long," Andor said to them. "There will be more Shadowstalkers on the way. Sigrid, you and Tahl take first watch, but only for an hour. Then Soot and I will relieve you. We leave as soon as Seppo reaches us."

Eva tried to imagine the hulking golem running through the trees, hurtling over boulders and streams. He was fast and did not get tired, but still couldn't keep up with the gryphons. At least, Eva thought, no Smelterborn would reach them before Seppo did — he outpaced even the swiftest golems.

Everyone settled down. Eva rested her back against Fury, using his warmth to keep away the chill since they couldn't risk a fire. Unable to even think about sleep, she turned the Wonder over and over in her hands. The light faded from white to pink and gold before at last settling on sky blue.

Eva's mind emptied and she stared into the depths of the stone. The light looked familiar. Eva thought and thought but her exhausted, grief-stricken mind couldn't place where she'd seen it before. Just on the edge of recollection, the memory left her frustrated and irritated. Eva stuffed the stone back beneath her chainmail.

A heartbeat later, something crashed through the undergrowth and everyone jumped to their feet, hands on their weapons. The sound of snapping tree limbs and iron boots stomping on rock continued until Seppo emerged from the brush. Eva breathed out a sigh of relief and lowered her sword.

"Hello!" Seppo said in his usual cheerful voice. "It would seem I have found you."

"You think?" Soot grumbled. "Where've you been? We've waited for hours!"

"I'm sorry," Seppo said without a hint of sarcasm, plucking a twig from between two armored plates. "I had a rather hard time keeping up on foot and was not informed of a meeting location."

Eva snorted. The others grinned as Soot's face turned red and he ground his teeth together. If he understood he'd made a joke, Seppo's bright blue eyes showed no sign.

Seppo's bright blue eyes.

Eva stared for a moment before it clicked into place.

"That's it!" she shouted, yanking the Wonder stone out again. Everyone looked at Eva like she'd lost her mind as she held the chain above her head, dangling in front of Seppo's face. The colors inside the stone swirled and changed, no different from any other time. Nothing else happened.

"Eva, maybe you need to get some rest…" Tahl said, lowering her arms with a gentle push of his hand.

Eva jerked away but was too excited to be angry. "Listen to me! The light doesn't affect Seppo like it does the Smelterborn." The stone turned the same shade of blue as the golem's eyes and she shook it in front of Tahl and the rest, who still appeared to be deciding if she'd lost her mind.

"Look! It's the same color! Why did I not think of it before? What if Seppo made this Wonder to help defeat the Smelterborn?"

A few uncertain looks passed between the group but Eva could tell they weren't convinced.

"That might be true but, like you said, it has no effect on him," Ivan said. "Your Wonder is a useful tool for fighting the Smelterborn but… that seems to be about it."

Eva turned and thrust the Wonder at Seppo once more, determined to prove them wrong. The golem stared at the lights as they changed from gold to pink and the familiar sapphire hue but, as Ivan said, nothing happened. Inside, Eva felt her excitement evaporate and her face burned with embarrassment.

She sighed. "I guess I just —"

"May I see that?"

Seppo held out his hand, still staring at Eva's Wonder. She shrugged. "Guess so."

The stone's golden chain slithered through her fingers and the Wonder made a soft ping, landing in Seppo's metal palm. Seppo closed his iron fingers around it.

In the next instant, blinding light burst from between his clenched fist. Eva and the others stumbled backward, raising hands to cover their throbbing eyes. Seppo let out a grating moan like rusted metal screeching together and collapsed to the ground. It was impossible to look at the golem or the stone, and Eva felt the warm glow of the Wonder cover her entire body as if a fire burned in Seppo's hand.

"Put it down, you iron idiot!" Soot shouted. "Drop it!"

The light winked out as soon as the stone fell from Seppo's grasp. No one spoke. The golem looked around at them in apparent confusion and clambered to his feet, limbs quaking.

Eva blinked and squeezed her eyes shut, trying to get rid of the flashing spots in her vision. Her skull throbbed with the worst headache she'd ever felt.

"What in the tempest was that?" Sigrid said. "My head feels like it was split with an ax!"

"Has that happened before?" Andor asked.

Eva shook her head and wracked her memory. "I don't…Seppo's never actually touched it before, not that I can remember anyway."

"He has once."

All eyes turned to Soot.

"Back at Palantis," the smith said. "Aleron and I found him laying there, didn't look like anything but an empty suit of armor. Aleron thought he'd play a joke on the others and drop the stone inside the helm so it looked like it was glowing. The joke was on him — Seppo woke up, scared the feathers right off Aleron!"

"And you never bothered to tell anyone?" Ivan asked, incredulous.

Soot frowned at the Scrawl. "At first I didn't want that stone to put him back to sleep! In the years since I just kind of forgot about it."

"May I say something?"

Seppo picked up the Wonder by the chain, careful to not let the stone touch him, and handed it back to Eva. "Things are...clearer now.

"Talus was my name, I was an inventor of some kind. The First Forge... it was meant to be my greatest triumph but it failed." Seppo paused and heaved a sigh. "I-I was ashamed — my life's work was all for naught. In my agony, I threw myself into the fires of the forge, to end my existence."

Eva felt a cold chill run down her back. Memories of her battle against the first Smelterborn in the depths of the Gyr resurfaced and she shuddered to remember the dark blood magics she'd witnessed.

"I awoke in the flames, but I was not burning," Seppo continued. "When I emerged from the First Forge, I found I had succeeded. I was a golem, my soul protected by an enchanted iron body that would never age. I was immortal!"

Eva took a step back, sensing a change in Seppo's voice she'd never heard before. He sounded...harsher now, and she sensed the madness that had been lurking in the shadows of his triumph.

"What happened?" Soot asked in a hoarse voice. Eva wasn't sure if she wanted to know.

Seppo shook his iron head and his fists clenched in frustration. "I-I am not sure. It is all so fragmented. Something — Illmaren, no!"

They waited in silence until Seppo regained his composure. The golem's broad shoulders sank and he bowed his head. Eva didn't want to ask, seeing how much pain the memories caused her lifelong friend and guardian. But she knew she had to.

"Who was Illmaren, Seppo?" she asked, mustering an empathetic tone. "Please — I know it hurts, but we need to know."

"He was my apprentice," Seppo said, voice flat. "He...he died in the Forge. Afterward...I am not sure. There are large chunks missing. I fled Palantis. It was at that time the Smelterborn were created. I was angry — someone corrupted my creation! I returned, some years later... to destroy the First Forge.

"By now there were very few Palantines left. I led them through Palantis…there were golems everywhere. No! My friends! Fire! Smoke! *Ogunn!*"

A familiar darkness seized Eva, the same hopelessness that had dogged them on the Endless Plains. She had never heard the name spoken before but somehow she knew, knew this was the evil they faced.

"It was he who corrupted the First Forge," Seppo said. "The Smelterborn were his vile design. We…fought. The Palantines stood no chance. We failed… The next thing I remembered was being awakened by Soot in the ruins."

An oppressive silence permeated the forest clearing. The humans looked at one another but no one dared break the quiet.

"So what do we do now?" Wynn asked, unable to contain herself any longer.

"We go back to the city," Andor said. "And try to save as many people as we can."

"There is another chance," Seppo said. He gestured to Eva's Wonder and then turned to Soot. "Do you have the other?"

Soot nodded and reached for a pouch tied to his belt, extracting the Dark Wonder. The two stones glittered in each other's presence as if vying for control, Eva's flashing golden light and the other pulsing blood red from the runes carved in its ebony surface. "Adelar gave it to me for safe keeping. Haven't let the sky-cursed thing out of my sight since we left the city, why?"

"I used Mistress Evelyn's stone to power the First Forge," Seppo explained. "It's twin is the dark stone. Ogunn killed my apprentice and stole it from him, corrupting it and the First Forge to birth his Smelterborn.

"It is what Ogunn has sent his army of golems for. I am sure of it. He knows I am awake and that he is vulnerable while it is in our possession. With both stones, I believe I could destroy my creation for good and, in turn, the Smelterborn."

"That's all well and good," Andor said. "But unless you can take your forge apart from here, it doesn't change the fact that hundreds of golems are marching on Gryfonesse right now. The Scrawls will have sealed the pass, but that isn't going to stop them forever."

"No," Eva said, "but it could buy us some time. If the Smelterborn can sense the Dark Wonder and it's taken *back* to Palantis, perhaps they'll follow."

Everyone but Seppo stared at her like she'd grown a second nose.

"There's hundreds and hundreds of miles between us and Old Palantis," Soot said. "And each one of them has a dozen different ways to kill a person. And am I the only one who realizes Seppo can't fly? It would take months to even reach the coast on foot!"

"And the First Forge will likely be well-protected," Ivan said. "With golems, yes, but powerful rune wards as well, I imagine. It would take an army to even reach Palantis!"

Eva shook her head. "We don't need an army. A small group has a better chance of sneaking on the island without being noticed; like my father did."

"You're crazier than I am!" Sigrid laughed. "That's a death wish! We don't stand a chance!"

"It can be done," Seppo said. "The Smelterborn will not know for certain where the Dark Wonder is — especially the closer we are to Palantis. The odds of survival are not in our favor, however."

Wynn shook her head. "You must've lost a couple of screws. Sigrid's right, that's the craziest thing I've ever heard of!"

"So crazy it might work," Tahl said in a low voice. "And it's the best chance we have, as far as I can tell."

"But you are the queen now!" Chel said to Eva, placing a hand on her arm as if to beg her to stay. "You cannot do this."

Eva looked at Andor. So far her uncle hadn't said a word, just watched with a brooding expression on his face while the others talked.

"What would you have me do?" she asked.

"I would have you return to Gryfonesse and defend your people," he said, followed by a long pause. "But as Chel says, you are queen now. The choice is yours."

Thinking of all the innocents in Rhylance gave Eva pause. There was no easy answer. The chances of them making it all the way to the First Forge, let alone finding and successfully destroying it, was a long shot. But so was defending Gryfonesse from the Smelterborn, especially after what they'd seen in the Talon.

"You asked what I would have you do," Andor said, noticing her hesitation, "Adelar would probably say the same. But you aren't my daughter and you aren't Adelar's daughter." He paused and a grim smile spread across his face. "Your father would take the stones to the First Forge."

Eva couldn't help but give a small smile back before growing somber once more. "Then I would ask you, lord commander, to rally our troops and return to the city. Gryfonesse is your command now... I will go to the First Forge."

Looking around at her friends, their exhausted faces covered in dirt and streaked with sweat, Eva knew she couldn't ask any more of them. Especially not this. "If —"

"Oh, come on," Sigrid said, rolling her eyes. "You already dragged me and Ivan and Chel all over hell and back once. You know we're coming."

Ivan looked at Sigrid like he'd seen a ghost. He opened his mouth to say something but then seemed to think better of it and nodded. "I'm with you, Eva," he said in a quiet voice.

"I am with you as well, sister," Chel said.

"And the only reason I didn't go last time is because you didn't give me the chance!" Wynn stepped up with the rest, looking determined to fight anyone who told her no.

Eva's eyes met Tahl's.

"I should have gone with you last time," he said. "I won't make that mistake again."

That left only Soot.

"The last time I told you I was going east, you said you wouldn't go back for anything in the world," Eva said. Aside from Seppo, who only had partial memories, Soot was the only one who'd been to Palantis before. Eva knew she needed her foster father, as much for his quiet strength as his knowledge.

"You're going to drive me into an early grave," Soot muttered in his best grumpy tone. "I reckon this is the only reason worth going back to that sky-cursed hole. Guess that means we're coming too, eh Seppo?"

The golem nodded. "I am the cause of all this. We will come with you, Evelyn, and help you destroy the First Forge."

Eva looked at them each, in turn, heart swelling for her friends and loved ones.

"Let's save the world."

Chapter 14

With no sleep and a few rations they'd scrounged together, the group set off at sunset, now heading south. Although the gryphons disliked flying in the dark, walking on the ground under an enclosed canopy of pines was worse. They took to the air, circling above as the riders walked along in the dark.

With no idea how far the Smelterborn were behind them, Eva remained on edge for any sign of attack, such as a snapping stick, a looming shadow between the trees or the crunch of an iron boot on rock, but the forest remained silent. One advantage — if you could call it that — of being chased by iron golems, she'd realized after several encounters, was that suits of armor couldn't move with much stealth. Not even the Shadowstalkers or scouts were quiet enough for gryphon, or even human, ears to miss. Nevertheless, they walked with hands on weapons, ready for an ambush at any moment.

Gray morning revealed they'd kept their intended course, holding the Windswept mountain range to their left. Despite a night of clambering over boulder fields and doing their best not to tumble down steep ravines, they'd made decent progress. But progress came with a price. Eva felt exhaustion dragging at her, tripling the weight of her chainmail until her arms, legs, neck, and back felt like she carried a Smelterborn's iron shell, not her lightweight armor.

Thankfully, they had Seppo to clear the way for them. The golem hefted broken branches and rocks blocking their way, tirelessly blazing a trail through even the toughest terrain. In the growing daylight, Eva could see twigs, pine needles and dirt caught between the golem's plates or held fast by blotches of sap.

The golem let out the closest sound he could make to distaste and tried scrubbing himself to rid his armor of the sticky substance.

"What a mess," Seppo said flinging the handful of rock and sand away in disgust. "I'll be in need of a good scouring and oiling when this is done."

"Yeah, yeah," Soot said. "We really feel for you."

The rest of them had just as many twigs sticking out of their armor, but also enjoyed a host of cuts and scrapes — collateral of blundering through the pines in the dark. As tired as they'd been back in the meadow, Eva thought they resembled walking corpses now. The dark rings under their eyes were more pronounced, giving their features a sunken, skeletal look. Eva could only imagine what she would see peering into a looking glass.

Seppo found a small stream and the humans did their best to clean up after drinking deep and refilling their water skins in the frigid runoff. Passing around what was left of their rations helped sate everyone's growling stomachs. Eva didn't relish the task of foraging in the mountains in springtime when most plants had yet to flower and wild animals had picked the remnants of last year's bounty clean.

"Looks like it's back to dried meat and roots soon," Sigrid said around a mouthful of the last of her biscuit. "Seems like we just got off this yesterday. If I'd have known that, I would have eaten better when I had the chance."

"Pretty sure my belt thinks it was just yesterday," Ivan said, tugging at his waist. "I swear, if I make it through this I'm going to get so fat I can hardly walk!"

"There are worse things to eat," Chel said. "Especially when nothing is all there is."

Eva silently agreed with Sigrid and Ivan. Although it felt like an age ago, she reminded herself they'd just spent weeks on the Endless

Plains, fleeing the Smelterborn west. Now, with barely any time to recover during the flurry of war, they were doing it all over again, in the opposite direction.

"It will be better this time," Chel added. They all looked at her, but she gave no answer.

"How in the name of the sky will it be better this time?" Sigrid asked, incredulous.

"Oh, I think I can answer that," Seppo cut in. "I believe what the Juarag-Vo woman means is that this time, the chances of any of you surviving to make the return journey are so small that your suffering will likely be over sooner than later."

Chel stared at Seppo, a faint look of horror on her face. "That is not what I meant at all!"

"Alright, alright, enough gabbing," Soot said. "Seppo you get to take watch — all night, every night. Since the rest of us need sleep, how about we all pipe down and try for some, eh?"

While the gryphons went off to hunt — it'd been almost two days since they'd eaten — Eva and the rest hunkered down beneath a large pine. The old tree sat on a short rise overlooking the beginnings of a gorge cut by a torrent of water below. Most likely it had been snow the day before, melted off the mountains just above the tree line.

Eva closed her eyes and focused on the sound of the rushing stream, trying to clear her mind using a meditation technique she'd learned from Ivan. Soon, she felt herself drifting away and finally fell into a deep slumber.

Seppo woke them a short time later — Eva didn't know how long they'd slept but it wasn't long enough. Still, she felt the edge of her fatigue blunted and stretched her sore muscles. It was midday, overcast and dreary, but the clouds were far above and didn't look to hold rain or snow.

Soot gathered them around a bare patch of dirt and began sketching out a rough map of Altaris on the ground with the end of a stick.

"Here we are, about halfway down the Windswepts," he said, drawing a series of vertical arrow shapes. In any other situation, Eva might've commented on how childlike the drawings looked, but she held her tongue and focused on the crude map.

"The Talon is the largest and easiest pass, but there are some on the Rhylance Skrael border that we can take without too much problem," Soot marked these with a couple of Xs. "Once we cross the mountains, we'll take the same route as the last time, skirting below the Endless Plains through Ivan's country."

"It may still be winter in Skrael," Ivan cautioned. "Our cold season lasts longer than it does farther north."

"We'll just have to deal with it," Soot said. "There's not time to swing back around to the north, not without losing weeks and any ground we've gained on the Smelterborn."

"South it is, then," Eva agreed.

To the right of his mountains, Soot drew a big circle marking Skrael and the other southern lands. "Most of the country through here is hills, mountains, and forest, much like this, if I remember right. Good news is spring should be well on by the time we get into the highlands." He made several more markings even farther to the right. "Beyond that, we'll eventually drop into the river country and then hit the woodlands and the ruins of the Palantine Empire. From there, it's a roughly northeast shot to the coast. We follow it until we see the island and there you have it."

He sat back and folded his arms over his broad chest. Looking at the rough map, it seemed the simplest plan in the world. What the scratches in the dirt didn't show were the miles and miles of rough country, spring storms and Smelterborn they'd face, nor did it take into account the fact they'd be traveling slowly, unable to fly beyond what Seppo could walk in a day.

"It's a good plan," Eva said. "But what about when we get to the island? How can we evade the Smelterborn?"

"We may have an advantage in our favor," Seppo said.

They looked at the golem expectantly but he stared at the mountain peaks as if he'd forgotten about the conversation. Soot smacked him on the breastplate. "Focus, rust bucket!" he growled. "What are you talking about?"

"The First Forge gives the Smelterborn life," Seppo said. "And Ogunn has overstretched his army to recover the Dark Wonder. It may be that if they have sensed the stone is moving east that they will abandon the attack on Rhylance and return to Palantis, lest they become inanimate."

"So it's a race to see who can make it to the island first," Tahl said.

Seppo nodded. "In a way, yes."

"The good news is old Seppo here is faster than your run of the mill golem," Soot said, thumping the golem's chest plate again, pride apparent in his voice. "It'll be close, but there's a chance, at least."

"No time to waste then," Sigrid said, standing. "The sooner we get through storming Skrael, the better."

The weather grew wetter and colder the farther south they traveled. Frequent spring storms poured buckets of rain and often turned into giant, wet snowflakes that left them soaked to the bone and shivering. While the gryphons and their riders flew overhead, Seppo ran along beneath them, bounding over the roughest terrain at a pace impossible for a human. When the gryphons needed rest from the additional riders, Soot, Chel, and Ivan walked with Seppo. Even with the benefit of flight, the days grew long and tiring.

Just as Soot promised, the highlands of Skrael proved to be fierce and unforgiving. Sigrid, Tahl, Eva, and Wynn took turns scouting ahead in pairs, a method that helped them circumvent a numbers of ravines and canyons that would have otherwise added days to their journey. Although the humans could be safely ferried across through the air, all four gryphons combined could barely lift Seppo off the ground and then only until the ropes broke from the weight.

After three more days travel, Soot found the pass they were looking for, a high scree field far above the tree line between two snow-capped peaks where nothing but moss and lichen grew. They passed between the two mountains peaks in somber silence. At the top of the pass, Soot pointed out a large pile of rocks off to one side of the narrow trail.

"I'll be stormed!" he said with a rare chuckle. "We piled those up as a waypost marker on the last trip. Can't believe they're still standing — never thought I'd ever see them again."

Eva walked over to the tower of rocks and saw a large flat stone leaning against the boulder forming the foundation of the pile. It was the size of a table, with names carved into the rock by rune magic. Eva knelt down and ran her fingers over the letters. She recognized several, including Wayland — Soot's given name — Andor, Uthred, and Celina.

She paused before reading the last out loud. Eva traced her fingers over the grooves cut into the stone. "Aleron Vakarin, Expedition Captain."

Soot snorted, but a small smile played on his gruff features. "That cocksure young idiot. He gave that title to himself. Drove everyone else half-crazy trying to get us to address him as captain. It was only a joke — I think. Sometimes you couldn't tell with Aleron."

Eva closed her eyes and tried to imagine her father and the rest of the expedition standing right where they were now, full of excitement and anticipation for what lay ahead. Little had they known they'd waken an evil capable of destroying all Altaris. Not to mention alter the course of Eva's family forever. At that point had Adelar already begun courting her mother, attempting to steal his brother's betrothed? Were the seeds of their love already planted, waiting to grow? Was she torn, even then, between the two brothers?

Regardless of the aftermath, Eva felt encouraged to stand in her father's footsteps. Perhaps, she mused, she'd been meant to reach this crossroads all her life.

The southeastern tail of the Windswepts changed from barren gray rock to pine forests far darker and taller than those on the western side of the mountains or to the north. Journeying beneath the ominous boughs felt to Eva as if she'd stepped into another world. The thick canopy made it hard for the parties on the ground and air to stay in contact with one another. If anything were to happen, she doubted the gryphons would be able to find a place to land through the thicket of branches.

Ivan, on the other hand, seemed rejuvenated by the sharp scent of pine mixed with the earthy tones of the wet loam. When they descended into the trees he paused and sucked in a deep breath of air, tilting his head back and spreading his arms.

"Smells like home, doesn't it?" he asked Sigrid.

Sigrid frowned and, for a moment, Eva thought Ivan would be sporting a black eye. "The Gyr is home. This is just another sky-cursed forest."

A tense silence followed. Soot and Chel shot Eva a questioning look. What they didn't know was that Sigrid was Bersi — a Scrawl who couldn't use rune magic. Given Sigrid's natural inclination for violence, it wasn't a sore spot Eva wanted them to prod at. She shot both Soot and Chel an expression to drop it.

Ivan, knowing full well Sigrid's background, chose to let the subject fall into an awkward silence as well. "Well, uh, I've missed it anyway."

"Good for you," Sigrid snarled. "Now can we keep moving or do you want to sniff around some more?"

Before anyone could answer, she stormed off, hacking any unfortunate foliage that crossed her path. Her sour mood continued for the rest of the day and, after seeing to Sven and cleaning her weapons, Sigrid curled up in her blanket and went to bed. Eva waited until her friend's snores punctuated the night before allowing Ivan to explain to Soot and Chel.

"Almost all Skraelings are born with some affinity for rune magic," Ivan said, "but not all. These we call Bersi — it translates to something like 'unblessed' in your language. Most lead normal lives, but some of the more backward, highlands clans consider Bersi to be a curse from the Muse Mother."

Chel nodded in understanding. She herself was an outcast of the Juarag and had grown up in a band of misfits called Juarag-Vo, or tribeless.

"It's not something Sigrid talks about," Eva said.

"I've known Sigrid the longest out of any of us," Tahl said. "And trust me, this is the last thing you want to talk to her about. We were in the same class of cadets and there were some other children who made fun of her for her rune markings and being a Scrawl. She sent them all to the infirmary on our second day."

Eva winced, recalling a beating Sigrid had given her when she was a green recruit.

"Like it or not, we might run into some other Scrawls before we make it to the river lands," Ivan said, glancing across the fire at Sigrid's still, snoring outline. "I hope she behaves herself — the clans out in the wilds aren't as… civilized as the Scrawls you've all dealt with before."

They continued over miles of rolling hills, steep mountain expanses, and thick forest. The land east of the Windswepts and south of the Endless boasted crueler country than Eva imagined. Bellowing rivers of snowmelt cut through huge cliffs where mounds of snow still clung to the shadows. The cold, cruel spring storms lashed them with sleet, and whenever the pale sun managed to fight through the clouds, it offered little warmth or light.

Each day blended together and the travelers forged a common understanding between one another. Ivan, Chel, Eva, and Sigrid, having already spent over half a year together, were used to one another's annoying habits and quirks. Likewise, Sigrid and Tahl, often companions on various Windsworn missions with Lord Commander Andor, got along fine. But the rest, particularly Soot and Sigrid, butted heads like a pair of mountain sheep.

The pair argued over everything until it drove Eva crazy just seeing them tense up and glower at one another. When Soot wanted to continue on for the day, Sigrid thought they should stop and hunt. When Sigrid wanted to change course, Soot wanted to keep their current direction. Constant reminders of her birthplace left Sigrid snarling and spitting like a wet cat. At last, Eva could take no more.

"Enough!" she yelled just as it looked like they were about to come to blows over the best place to build the night's fire. "I don't care how the two of you work it out but the rest of us can't stand any more of this!"

Sigrid bared her teeth at Soot. Eva knew her friend had no hesitation trying the bigger, stronger man on for size. Soot, sometimes sharp-tongued but usually the last to resort to physical conflict, looked just as ready to give Sigrid a sore rear end. After several tense moments, however, the two relented, mumbling unintelligible apologies. Although it was in a worse spot, Eva had Ivan build the fire in a third location different from both Sigrid's and Soot's. Their meager meal didn't help to improve anyone's outlook.

"Now the snow is melting we might find a Scrawl village or camp to trade with," Ivan said. Everyone glanced at Sigrid, but she seemed completely focused on putting an even finer edge on her favorite ax and didn't notice or pretended not to hear Ivan.

The thought of eating something besides stale, brick-like bread, dirty roots and fire-blackened meat sounded too good to pass up. In the morning and over the next few days, Eva sent Sigrid and Wynn to scout out any sign of a Scrawl village in their somewhat immediate vicinity. She hoped some time in the sky with Sven would improve her friend's disposition. But when they returned in the afternoon, Eva could tell right away they bore bad news.

"Well, we found someone," Sigrid said. "But it sure ain't Scrawls and I doubt they'll give us anything to eat."

"Who —" Eva started to ask. Before she could finish the question, Wynn cut in, eyes wide.

"Juarag!"

Chapter 15

A whole raiding party by the look of it," Wynn said. "Twenty warriors mounted on sabercats."

"That doesn't make any sense," Tahl said, frowning. "The Juarag stay on the plains or foothills —they don't hunt in the high country. Besides, I thought all of them had been pushed west by the Smelterborn?"

"This looks like a different tribe than the ones that were gathered on the frontier and on the Talon," Sigrid said. "All their war cats are black and gray, painted with red."

Eva turned to Soot for his input. The smith shrugged. "Might be nothing. They've been pushed out of their hunting grounds — could be they're just looking for fresh meat in the spring. If the Smelterborn are heading back east, some of the tribes might be returning to the plains."

Soot didn't sound convinced and somehow Eva didn't think that was the case, either. It made no sense for a raiding party of Juarag to just happen to be in the highlands near them. By the look of it, Chel thought the same thing as well.

"There were rumors," she said, "that some tribes allied with the Smelterborn. Such an act would be beyond dishonorable, however."

Eva's stomach twisted.

"How far away are they?" she asked Sigrid and Wynn.

"Ten miles northwest, at most," Sigrid said. "They're moving in our direction, but I don't think they saw us. We were flying pretty high up and had some cloud cover."

"Nothing to do but keep an eye on them," Soot said. "Let's see what we can round up for dinner."

Over the next few days, Sigrid and Wynn continued observing the Juarag. It soon became apparent they were being loosely followed by the raiders — their path took a turn east, running parallel to Eva and her companions. At last, Eva decided she needed to see the band for herself. She and Tahl followed Sigrid and Wynn on their gryphons, flying high as they could given the elevation and cold.

Once Sigrid pointed out the parties, they landed in the crags, each on their own perch and observed the group far below.

Just as Sigrid said, the group looked to be made entirely of warriors, armed with an array of weapons, including spears, bows, clubs, and hide shields — weapons for war, not hunting. They traveled two wide, the black and gray war cats picking their way through a boulder field with ease, despite their size.

"They're moving quick enough they might be able to head us off," Eva said to Fury, huddled down against his neck to stay warm. "Almost as fast as Seppo... Do you think —"

Fury let out an unexpected hiss, drawing Eva from her thoughts. And then she saw them.

Almost impossible to make out against the dark rocks were two Smelterborn, a scout and one of the Shadowstalkers, judging by the golem's narrow, oblong head. The Shadowstalker carried a long staff in his hands that ended in a twisted shape Eva couldn't make out at their distance. The golem raised its staff and held it out before him, moving it from side to side. After a long moment, the golem turned all the way around directly facing the ledge where the gryphons and their riders perched.

Eva's insides turned cold as the Smelterborn stared up at the rocks they were hidden in for several long moments. At last, it shook its head and continued off in the same direction they'd been heading, towards Seppo, Soot, and Chel.

"It's torn between the two stones," Eva said, half to herself and half to Fury. "It doesn't know whether to head toward us or Soot." The gryphon stared at the Smelterborn, ears pinned back against his feathered head as if he hadn't heard Eva.

The Wonder stone felt like ice against her skin and Eva reached a trembling hand inside her shirt to wrap her fingers around it. At her touch, the thing grew warm once more and shone with its regular array of colors.

"Put it away!" Sigrid hissed. Eva stuffed the chain and stone back under her tunic and saw the black Smelterborn had paused again, staff held out in their direction once more.

That was all Eva needed to see. "Come on," she said as soon as the golem turned away after several long moments. "Let's get out of here."

They left the crags one by one, not wanting to draw attention of the entire group of gryphons taking flight at once. To further confuse the Juarag and their Smelterborn trackers, Eva led them in a circle around the backside of the mountain peak, the opposite way they'd flown in from.

"They are hunting us," Chel said when they returned to camp and related what they'd seen.

No one else spoke as the realization sank in. Eva felt like a fool for believing they wouldn't be followed and chastised herself for not being more careful.

"What if we ambush them?" Sigrid suggested. "They won't be expecting that."

"We'd lose too much time, not to mention we're outnumbered," Eva said. "I don't want to risk it. Besides, there could be more out there."

If the previous silence had been discouraging, this one was downright dreadful. "They could be *everywhere*," Wynn said in a hushed voice.

"Stick to the plan," Soot said, his booming voice striking them out of their despair like a hammer knocking away slag. "We'll keep scouting, travel fast and make sure no one goes anywhere alone."

They all agreed, although Eva could tell Chel and Wynn, in

particular, seemed less than comforted. But it seemed the best course to take or, as the Windsworn were apt to say, any perch in a storm. They'd simply have to move faster.

But Eva toyed with another idea as well — the Smelterborn and Juarag hunted the stones, her Wonder, and the one Soot carried. If she could manage to take the Dark Wonder from Soot without him noticing, she could lead their hunters away from the rest of the group...

Of course, she realized in the next moment, it wouldn't work. The First Forge couldn't be destroyed without Seppo's help and there was no way Seppo would go with her plan, nor could she escape the others with gryphons with Seppo on foot. Instead, Eva vowed to do everything to keep her friends safe. She thought back to her father's death just a few months before and told herself she would never let that happen again to someone else she loved.

Once more, they fell into a routine: scout and check the location and distance of the Juarag and Smelterborn, hunt for food, find a camp, repeat. The constant worry of their pursuers dogged Eva's thoughts, compounded with the constant need to stay dry and fed. As such, she felt an enormous amount of relief when they spotted a Scrawl camp not too far ahead. Ivan, Tahl, and Eva went to greet them. Sigrid naturally elected to stay behind, scowling while she put new edges on her array of knives and axes.

The Scrawl camp sat on the edge of a large meadow, shared by a large, mirror-like pond. Eva and Tahl landed their gryphons on the opposite edge of the clearing to avoid undue cause for alarm. Although the Scrawls were allies with Rhylance, it hadn't been many years since the nations had been at war, fighting over territory. Some of the more remote clans, Ivan said, still held plenty of grudges against the gryphon people.

"Don't call them Scrawls," Ivan warned. "It doesn't bother most of us, but some of the remote clans find it extremely offensive and disrespectful to our language. Make sure you say it the right way: Skrael."

Eva was surprised to find the Scrawls living in skin tents similar to the Juarag. She reminded herself that long ago before the Sorondarans came to Altaris or the Palantine Empire reached its height, the ancestors of the Scrawls and Juarag were the same people. Although they also populated a few ancient cities, including the famous Library of Skaal, many still kept to their old nomadic lifestyles as druids.

A flurry of activity filled the camp once the clan saw them approaching. Two Scrawls, a man and woman tattooed with so many runes that their skin looked almost purple, walked toward them as they crossed the meadow. In spite of the chilly spring weather, the woman wore only a few strips of leather and cloth across her chest and a pair of leggings. The man was bare-chested and wore only leggings. They both walked barefoot across the sloppy marsh ground, seemingly unaffected by the bite of the cold mud. Both parties halted several paces from one another.

"You are a long way from home," the Scrawl man said. He clutched a twisted staff of gray wood in his hand, carved with runes and animal and plant totems. The woman stared at them without offering a greeting, her cold gray eyes passing over each of them in turn. Eva noticed the woman wore a silver ring, a Wonder judging by its craftsmanship, around her neck on a leather throng.

"Is there not war enough in your lands?" the woman asked, speaking in a voice as harsh as her expression. "I would have thought that would keep you from trespassing into ours."

"There is," Eva said, carefully choosing each word. Worshipers of language, everything said to the Scrawls had to be measured and selected with care. "And we are grateful for the rune masters that Skrael sent to help us defend our people."

"Flattering words, but they do not answer my question," the woman said.

"*Two pretty birds with travelers three,*" the man said in a singsong voice while he danced a little jig. "*What oh what do they want from me?*"

Eva shot Ivan a confused glanced but her friend just shrugged. "I've heard better," Ivan told the man. The Scrawl only gave a wide grin in response, leaving Eva with the impression he might be a few runes short of a book.

"We are traveling east to fight the golems," Eva said. "We are here to barter supplies from you for the days ahead. We also came to warn you — there are Juarag who have joined with the Smelterborn and they are in your mountains."

"Because you brought them here," the woman said in an accusing tone. She looked at Ivan and shook her head in disgust. "Why do you travel with these outsiders who trespass on our lands?"

"I am helping them defeat the Smelterborn," Ivan said, frowning back at her. "The golems are everyone's enemy."

"*From out of the west into the east.*" The Scrawl man sang again and resumed his shuffling dance. "*Can't fight the golems with nothing to eat.*"

"Quiet, Rhys!" the woman snapped before turning to the others. "We travel light to our spring camp and have little to trade. Then again, I doubt you have anything we want, either."

"Our gryphons can bring you fresh meat," Tahl said, gesturing back to Fury and his white gryphon, Carroc. Both creatures dug at the soft grass and sod across the meadow, clearly bored and eager to be gone.

"Ha!" the woman spat. "So you hunt from our lands and then offer to trade the meat back to us?"

"Please," Eva said. "Is there nothing we can give that you would like?"

The woman seemed to think for a long moment and then pointed to Eva's chest. "The relic around your neck would probably suffice."

Eva clutched at her neck, unsure of how the Scrawl woman even knew about her Wonder, which remained hidden underneath her tunic.

"I...I'm afraid that's not for trade," she said.

"*Pretty stones and blinking lights. What is the price to buy a life?*"

"Does he have anything useful to add to the conversation?" Ivan asked, his patience clearly running thin. "What is the name of your clan? When I next see the Elders, I would like to let them know who among us refuses their hospitality."

The woman shifted into a stance Eva recognized as preparation for working rune magic. She barked out a couple of words and balls of fire burst to life, crackling in her hands. Eva reached for her sword and Ivan assumed a similar pose, the ground beneath them rippling like water boiling on a kettle. Sensing danger, the gryphons screeched from across the meadow, but luckily waited to be summoned.

"Enough!" Eva placed herself between the two Scrawls and held up her hands. Tahl came to her side at once, although how he thought he could protect her from rune magic with a blade, she didn't know. "I am Evelyn Vakarin, Queen of Rhylance, niece to the late King Adelar. I cannot give you this Wonder, but name your price and if it is fair and within my power, I will grant it."

The woman smirked and clamped her hands shut, snuffing out the balls of fire. "My, things have indeed changed in the outside world since the season darkened with winter."

"If you will not trade with us, we will be on our way," Eva said, tired of the woman's hostility.

"I never —"

A gryphon's scream split the sky to the west causing them all to spin around in alarm. Eva spotted Chel and Sigrid winging toward them on Sven, followed close behind by Wynn and Soot astride Lucia. Moments later, Seppo burst from the tree line on the opposite side of the pond, running at full stride.

"What is going on?" The Scrawl woman hissed, stepping back and summoning another ball of fire into her hand. Even Rhys looked alarmed and began muttering under his breath, hands twisting as he worked his own kenning.

"They are with us!" Eva said, hoping to avoid another conflict. "They mean you no harm, I promise!"

Sigrid landed between the humans and the other gryphons and ran toward them, not waiting for the others.

"It was a trap!" she shouted. "There are more Juarag and Smelterborn coming from the east — they're only a few miles away!"

Chapter 16

Behind them, the Scrawl woman cursed and pointed a finger at one of the rune markings on Sigrid's forehead. "What have you and this Bersi brought upon us?"

Sigrid's eyes narrowed and her nostrils flared. Eva recognized the look on her friend's face and blocked Sigrid's view of the Scrawl woman before they were fighting Scrawls in addition to Juarag and Smelterborn.

"How many are there?" Eva asked, forcing Sigrid to meet her eyes. She glanced at the Scrawl woman, half-expecting her head to be torched by a fireball.

"Too many," Sigrid said. "While you were gone, I thought I'd scout out ahead — Soot couldn't remember which river it was we needed to follow — that's when I saw them. At least a dozen Smelterborn — and I'm guessing these ones are fresh from Palantis — plus a score of Juarag, all on sabercats."

"Begone from here, fight your battles elsewhere!" the Scrawl woman shouted raising both hands, which glowed with rising flames. "My clan wants no part of this!"

"The ones we knew about are heading this way too," Sigrid said, lowering her voice so only Eva could hear her. "No way they'll pass by this bunch — the pickings are too easy. If this witch doesn't want us here then I say we leave. We can evade both parties if we swing farther south, but we have to leave now."

Eva looked at the Scrawl's camp on the edge of the meadow. The rest of the clan watching the proceedings seemed to include only a dozen men and women in their prime. The majority consisted of old ones and young children. A brief image of sabercats and Smelterborn tearing through the camp made up Eva's mind.

"We brought them here," she said. " Even if we're not welcome, I'm not going to leave these people to be slaughtered because of us."

"Forget them," Sigrid hissed fighting to keep her voice down. "We're the ones that will be slaughtered!"

Eva shook her head. "I can't."

"Then go and get yourself killed for these ungrateful savages, but I won't!" Sigrid balled her hands into fists and stalked off toward Sven. She made it all the way to the gray gryphon's side before letting out a roar and hurtling her favorite ax into the soft ground.

"Tempest take you, Eva," she said, followed by a string of more severe profanities. "You're going to be the death of me."

"The Bersi is right," the Scrawl woman said and spat again at their feet. "We do not need your help!"

"They will kill you all," Eva said. "Together, we can defeat them. Apart, we may both die."

The woman sneered and spun around to return to her camp but the man Rhys grabbed her shoulder. They spoke in hushed, angry tones too quiet to overhear for several moments. At last, the woman turned to the gryphon riders, still scowling.

"I do not like it, but Rhys is correct," she said, forcing each word out like it was poison. "We are together in this, like it or not."

Ivan extended a hand. "Your word?"

Eva knew no matter how much the Scrawl woman despised them, if she agreed, then she could be trusted. She remembered Ivan telling her once that each clan had a word, sacred to them. If Eva had asked for such a thing, the woman would have probably struck her down at once.

The woman's eyes widened in shock at Ivan's request. "You dare —"

Before she could say anything more, Rhys grasped Ivan's hand and muttered something in his ear. Ivan repeated something back — his own word, Eva guessed — and the two nodded.

"Bound by word," Rhys said.

"Bound in voice," Ivan replied.

Eva had taken the man for a simpleton, one of the rune-addled whose mind had been twisted by the magic, but he seemed anything but now.

"We have a safe place to send those who cannot fight," the man said. "Ferike will ready the warriors."

The woman, Ferike, looked less than pleased that the man had shared her name with them but ran off nonetheless to prepare her people.

"Is there better ground we can meet them on?" Soot asked, gazing around. The meadow wasn't bad — but it left them exposed on all sides. At least they could see them coming — the thought of facing the Juarag and Smelterborn in the trees, where the gryphons would be all but useless between the close trunks and boughs filled Eva with dread.

"Not that we have time to find," Tahl said. "We'll have to make do with what we have here."

The Scrawl camp dissolved in the space of a few minutes. The young and old melted away into the trees and the defenders selected a position with their backs to the pond. Although it left without a path of retreat, the water also protected their backs the best they could hope for in the given surroundings.

A short time later, Ferike and Rhys returned, with just over a dozen rune workers ranging from teens to older adults following them. They approached Eva's group with caution, especially the gryphons and Seppo. The friendly golem, on the other hand, seemed keen to meet the Scrawls.

"Delightful!" he exclaimed. "It's always a pleasure to work with someone who knows their way around the runes, even if you people are a bit... rudimentary compared to the Palantines. When the fighting begins, just remember I'm on your side!"

He finished with a short, metallic laugh that sounded a bit nervous.

Eva couldn't help but notice how the golem's personality continued to grow the closer they got to Palantis.

"We'll put you lot behind us," Soot told the Scrawls, gesturing to the edge of the water where a string of last year's cattails stalks stood dry and lifeless. "Hopefully we can hold them off while you do your work."

Ferike nodded and the rest of the Scrawls walked past them, careful to keep from touching any of the riders or meeting their eyes.

"I'm not sure we're all on the same side," Tahl muttered to Eva once they'd passed.

Eva didn't know what to say — the familiar sickness that always plagued her before a battle had crept up. She flexed her torso to keep her rolling stomach from sickening further and thought back briefly to all the fights she'd been in. None, not the Hippiriot on the plains, the Smelterborn on the plateau or the great battle at the Talon had begun with worse odds than this one. She'd been on patrols that had driven off Juarag raiders and had witnessed the brute strength and ferocity of the sabercats. Without question, the beasts were physical equivalents to gryphons.

They'd chosen not to fly during the battle to better protect the Scrawls and to make the gryphons less of a target for the Juarag's bows and throwing spears. Eva felt very alone and vulnerable on the ground, even with her comrades around her. She shifted her attention to Wynn, who looked even worse on the outside than Eva felt inside. She put on a brave face, catching Wynn's eye.

"Just stick with us and you'll be fine," Eva said, hoping the quaver didn't come through in her voice.

Wynn nodded and gritted her teeth, trying to show her best impression of Sigrid. The older, dark-haired woman seemed even more incensed with the Scrawls behind them. Sigrid locked her jaw and ground her teeth, eyes darting around, eager for the Smelterborn and Juarag to show themselves.

Eva glanced up but saw no sign of Fury or his comrades returning. The gryphons had gone off together to scout for the approaching enemy while the humans prepared their meager defense. She worried that they weren't back yet but told herself Fury and the others were smart enough to stay out of harm's way. On the plus side, the longer they were gone meant the farther away the Juarag and Smelterborn were.

"When they come, go for the golems first," Eva said. A few nodded and she felt a little more confident. "The Juarag and their sabercats are powerful, but they die like any other living thing. The Smelterborn, however, can only be brought down with strong rune magic or a strike through their helmet openings."

Before Eva could think of further advice or summon any encouraging words a gryphon scream split the air. Looking over the trees, she saw Fury and the other gryphons flying toward them at full speed.

Eva swallowed hard and tried to summon some steel to her voice. "Get ready!"

The air around them hummed from energy and elemental power as the Scrawls began their kennings. Soon the sound grew to a buzzing crackle. Eva had never felt so much power concentrated in one place. She glanced to her side at Soot. He stood calm and ready, a massive hammer hung loose in the grip of his good hand — her pillar of strength. Tahl gave her a crooked grin and a wink, spinning his sword in his grip. On Tahl's other side, Sigrid growled over the chanting of the Scrawls and banged an ax against her shield. Eva twisted her grip on her rune sword.

And then…

Nothing.

The Scrawls' combined chanting slowly died down to silence. Eva's hand burned and she loosened her grip on her weapon. The gryphons circled overhead — had they been mistaken?

Eva and the rest looked around, searching for any sign of movement on the edge of the forest. The trees were far enough away that the Juarag couldn't fire from the cover of the forest. With their numbers, Eva didn't see why they would do anything but a brute charge. The Smelterborn couldn't approach without causing a racket as they crashed through —

An enraged feline howl split the air. A heartbeat later, a wave of Juarag raiders mounted on sabercats burst from the treeline. Another cacophony of blood curdling screams sounded from the right as another band of raiders charged. The enormous cats pounded across the meadow as fast as galloping horses — a hasty count showed numbers closer to thirty in all.

Rolling with each bound of the giant felines beneath them, several Juarag drew back their bows, firing at random intervals at the bunched up group of gryphon riders and Scrawls. Some of the Scrawls shouted kennings to the wind and a breeze blew most of the arrows awry. A young Scrawl woman screamed in pain as one arrow found its mark, sinking deep in her leg. She let out a moan and collapsed clutching the wound.

Eva twisted her grip on her sword once more, unable to do anything but watch while the enemy drew closer. Time seemed to slow as the distance between them and the Juarag shrank. The Smelterborn followed close behind, the scouts and Shadowstalkers running faster than a man at full speed. Eva suddenly felt very small and vulnerable.

A massed shout burst from behind her and a hot wind nearly knocked Eva to the ground. The Scrawls' combined kennings of wind and fire struck the sabercats and their riders like a wall, frying several in the charge. The surviving beasts scattered as their riders fought to control the singed, uncontrollable felines. Thick smoke and an awful smell of burnt air and flesh filled the meadow.

But the Smelterborn passed through the wall of fire without pause. The other group of sabercats to the northwest continued unmolested. Eva braced herself for another kenning. None came. Twisting around, she saw half the Scrawls behind her with their hands on their knees, sucking in air.

For the moment, it was up to her and her friends.

Eva raised her sword, signaling the gryphons toward the other pack of sabercats closing in. Screaming their war cries, the gryphons dove toward the Juarag charge. At the same time, Seppo bounded toward them, roaring. Eva gritted her teeth and braced for the collision.

Chapter 17

Seppo and the gryphons crashed into the sabercats head-on. Running full speed, Seppo sank his shoulder into the chest of a cat, flipping beast and rider over backward. The gryphons dipped at the last moment, picking four riders out of the saddle with their talons. They rose, holding the flailing men tight in their grasp and only let go when they were at the peak of their second pass. All four men screamed before smacking into the ground where they laid unmoving.

Eva motioned to the other group of smoking sabercats and scorch-marked Smelterborn. Ferike nodded and took half of the Scrawls with her to press the attack. Letting loose a scream worthy of Sigrid, Eva led the rest in a charge toward the melee of Seppo, gryphons, sabercats and the Smelterborn.

Seppo fought like a machine of total destruction. As Eva and the rest neared, he punched a war cat on the side of the head. The beast went down in a heap. Without waiting to see if it was still alive, he leaped over the cat and locked arms with a Shadowstalker. Twisting, Seppo bored the Smelterborn to the ground. Another jumped on his back. With one hand, Seppo reached behind him and shed the smaller scout golem like a fly. It flew through the air, crashing into another sabercat.

Despite the defenders' vicious counter-attack, five of the Juarag regrouped and sprinted toward the humans from atop their sabercats. The gryphons struck again, this time hitting the raiders with closed, fisted talons scattering the Juarag line. Eva yelled and swung with all her might, burying her sword in the neck of a sabercat that was struggling to its feet. The beast let out a short yelp and jerked then went limp.

A lanky Juarag woman bowled into Eva's side and they both went down in a heap. Eva hit the ground hard. Her opponent's rotten furs reeked of spoiled meat and cat urine. Growling, Eva scrambled to get out from underneath the Juarag, her sword pinned beneath her. She rolled over, one hand fending off the woman's grasping hands, while she reached for the knife at her belt.

Wedging her knee against the woman's chest, Eva heaved and they broke apart, both rising with drawn knives. They circled one another for half a moment, Eva's gaze locked on the Juarag's hard, dark eyes.

Eva didn't hesitate. She lunged and the woman leaped to the side, falling for the trick. The Juarag's bone knife sliced past Eva's face. Planting her foot, Eva pivoted and buried her knife deep into the Juarag's shoulder. The woman screamed in agony and swung wildly, grazing the mail sleeve of Eva's armor. At the same time, Eva wrenched her knife free and sank it in the raider's side. But the blow brought Eva too close. Using the last of her strength, the Juarag slashed Eva across the stomach.

Eva felt the cut and gasped. The Juarag fell to the ground, bleeding from both wounds. In her state of shock, it took a moment for Eva to register the chainmail that had just saved her life. She stared down at the Juarag woman at her feet. Blood bubbled out of the woman's mouth as she hissed and choked.

A hand grabbed her shoulder, breaking Eva from her trance. She twisted around, knife raised and found Soot staring back at her. He'd lost his cap somewhere and had a long scratch down his bald head.

"You alright, girl?" he shouted.

Eva nodded and picked up her sword. She felt her breakfast rising and did not look back at the dying woman.

Seppo raged through Juarag and Smelterborn alike with the rest of them following in his wake. Eva ran after Soot, searching for the rest of her friends. Sigrid and Wynn fought close together, the younger girl giving a good account of herself against a larger Juarag man until Sigrid dispatched her opponent and came to Wynn's aid. Ivan and the Scrawls focused most of their attention on the Smelterborn, streaks of fire and ice shooting through the middle of the turmoil towards the golems.

A Shadowstalker sprinted toward Eva and she raised her sword to meet it. Just feet away, the ground boiled and tore open in a chasm, swallowing the Smelterborn whole. Moments later, it smoothed over as if nothing had ever happened. Eva caught sight of Ivan and he waved.

Searching for Tahl, Eva spotted him only a few yards away. Flanked by Carroc — who held his wing at a funny angle — the pair faced off against a Juarag warrior and his sabercat. Screeching, the cat pounced and Carroc met it, rearing up on his lion's legs. Long, dagger-like fangs and a wicked beak sought each the other's throat, their claws and talons scrabbling for advantage.

Tahl moved like lightning, slamming his shield into the cat rider's face and cutting deep into the man's chest with his sword. Carroc and the sabercat writhed atop the soft loam, throwing tufts of grass and mud into the air. A second sabercat launched itself at Tahl's back.

Eva screamed a warning, but it was too late. Tahl disappeared beneath the cat.

As Eva sprinted to Tahl's aid, a red streak flashed through the air beside her. Fury hit the sabercat full force in the side. Just as the two animals tangled together, Eva grabbed Tahl's arm, dragging him free of the awful fight.

Tahl's breath was shallow and he moaned, knocked half-senseless. Eva paused long enough to check him for serious injury then rushed to help Fury. Before she could, a sabercat leaped into her path.

The beast was huge, its brindled gray fur covered in scars. Sinking on its haunches, the cat pinned its ears back and let out a whining growl from deep in its throat.

Eva raised her sword in a guard stance and tried to brace her wobbling legs. Yelling, she swung at the beast. The cat hissed at the tip of Eva's sword flashing in front of his face. In a blur, it batted a massive paw at the blade. The edge caught, biting deep into the pads of the cat's foot.

Instinct alone saved Eva. The cat shrieked in pain and pounced. Even injured, the brindled sabercat moved like lightning, and Eva felt a whoosh of air as she dove to the side. She barely had time to collect herself as the cat smacked at her again, tearing Eva's sword from her grasp.

Weaponless, Eva froze. She dared not take her eye off the sabercat but knew she had nowhere to run and nothing to fight back with. The cat hissed and limped toward her. Eva took a faltering step backward and stumbled.

Soot came out of nowhere. Raising his hammer, the smith swung sideways, striking the sabercat before it changed focus from Eva. Twisting around to meet the new threat, the beast snapped at empty air with its long, horrible fangs.

Soot moved with a speed Eva wouldn't have believed possible. Bellowing, he smashed the hammer on the top of the cat's head with an awful crack.

The sabercat stumbled.

Thwack!

Eva's stomach rolled at the meaty sound of the hammer smashing through the beast's thick skull.

The sabercat collapsed with its mouth agape.

Soot tossed the hammer aside and rushed to Eva. Pulling her to her feet, they embraced, both of their chest's heaving from fear and exertion. Pulling away, Eva saw Fury worrying at his dead opponent's belly. Carroc let out a soft call, dripping blood from a ragged wing onto Tahl as he nudged his rider.

"Tahl!"

Eva ran to her beloved's side. Groaning, Tahl sat up, gently pushing away Carroc's beak.

"I'll live, I'll live," he said in between coughs.

The surviving Juarag and their cats ran for the trees. Heaps of iron marked the defeated Smelterborn torn apart by Seppo or struck down from the Scrawls' rune magic. A quick look told Eva all of her friends were alive, although she flinched at the number of Scrawls lying dead across the meadow.

They gathered together, the gryphons picking their way across the sodden, turned up ground. Fury, Sven, and Lucia all had various bites and cuts but none appeared too serious at first glance. Eva cringed at Carroc's limp wing. By the look of it, he wouldn't be able to fly until it was healed and rested for a day or two.

Wynn stumbled toward them in shock but, aside from a long cut down her arm, seemed whole. Spattered in gore, Eva couldn't tell with Sigrid, but she acted none the worse for wear. Chel limped on a swollen ankle. Eva hoped Ivan would be able to patch most of them up, once he stopped throwing up from the kenning sickness and rested.

The surviving Scrawls walked from one fallen clansmember to another, using the last of their strength to heal those not too far gone. Out of the injured, Eva doubted a third would make it, even with the help of magic. She squeezed her eyes shut as the glade started spinning.

Rhys joined them, blood splattered across his bare, tattooed chest. He looked exhausted, but even more pained as he surveyed his clan's dead.

"Ferike?" Ivan asked. The man shook his head and pointed to a pair of Scrawls pulling her body out from beneath a Shadowstalker.

"I am sorry," Eva said, bowing her head.

"We have rid the world of some of its evil," Rhys said. Eva couldn't believe the change from his former jovial tone. "Do not apologize. It was not you, but the Juarag and Smelterborn who brought this upon us."

"Should you ever find your way to Rhylance, come to the citadel in Gryfonesse," Eva said. "I know it will not replace the fallen, but I swear to repay this debt any way I can."

Rhys nodded but the hollow look never left his face. "I perceive that the road ahead will tax you enough."

To her left, Ivan winced.

"We must gather our dead and return to the rest of our clan," Rhys said. "Even so, we will give you what supplies we can spare. And our blessing."

The Scrawl raised his hands, palms facing them and swung them away from his body, chanting as he did so. Eva felt a small warmth run through her and nodded in thanks.

As the companions tended to their wounds and washed the gore of battle away, the Scrawls' dirges filled the meadow: songs of life and death that broke Eva's heart even though she didn't know any of their meaning.

A rough, untrained voice in their midst joined in. Eva looked in surprise at Sigrid, who stood next to Ivan and sang, eyes locked on the dead. No one spoke or moved as they continued, captivated by the raw, yet somehow lyrical, words and melody. When the song drew to an end, Sigrid bowed her head with the rest then turned and walked away, refusing to meet anyone's look.

When they were ready to depart, Ivan stopped at the edge of the meadow. He raised a hand in farewell to the Scrawls, who had gathered their dead on pine bough litters and, still singing, faded into the trees. Plumes of acrid smoke rose from the flaming piles of sabercats and Juarag, drifting into the still air. Using the last of their strength, the Scrawls buried the empty husks of the Smelterborn after Seppo piled them together.

Evening set in and a quiet, peaceful calm settled over the meadow. The wind changed and blew the smoke to the west, filling the air with the cool, clean scent of new life and spring.

"We brought this upon them," Eva said in a low voice. The guilt and grief weighed heavy on her heart.

"Destroy the First Forge, and we will avenge them," Soot said. "That's the only way to make sure they didn't die in vain."

Eva nodded but didn't feel any better.

Chapter

18

The following days stretched on, each longer than the last. The expanse of forest and mountains seemed never-ending. Even in the sky, there was no end in sight to the high country and Eva began to wonder if they would ever reach the eastern coast or Palantis.

Spirits remained downtrodden after the battle in the meadow. Most days, no one spoke more than a few muttered words and only when necessary. They continued scouting the surrounding country for Smelterborn and Juarag, but the land seemed devoid of any human life, even other Scrawl clans.

Before they'd gone their separate ways, Rhys provided them with a few supplies, dried fruits and hard cakes made from pounded acorn paste. After the terrible death toll the clan took from the battle, Eva was loath to take the food but knew they needed the added provisions. Although Rhys asked for nothing in return, the burden of guilt ended up a heavy cost nonetheless.

The weather grew cold, stormy and windy. The companions spent nights huddled around a flickering fire that Ivan constantly tended. Freezing and shivering. they ate their meager rations and whatever scrawny, winter-starved animals they dredged up in the high country.

Eva found some small relief lying in Tahl's arms each night. Since leaving the Talon, they hadn't spoken further about their engagement and no one else knew about it. Part of Eva wanted to tell them all, to talk with Tahl about their future together — a lone bright spot in a world of gray days and cold nights. Another part cautioned Eva not to get her hopes up, that the journey ahead was still long and fraught with peril.

The others huddled almost as close together as the lovers, a hodge-podge of cloaks, jackets, and pine serving as their shelter when the rains drizzled for days on end. One night, tossing and turning from half-dreams of the battle at the Talon and the more recent scrimmage in the forest glade, Eva could take no more.

Wrapping her cloak tighter around her, Eva joined Seppo on the edge of their camp. The friendly golem stood watch — a quiet sentinel in the wilds. The only sign of life in the golem came from his bright blue eyes peering into the forest night, searching for any sign of danger.

"You should be sleeping, mistress Evelyn," he said in a low voice.

"I thought you might like the company," Eva said. "It must get lonely standing watch all night alone."

Seppo's iron pauldrons rose in a shrug. "I am happy to do it."

"Are you…" Eva searched for the right word. "Nervous? Scared? For what's ahead, I mean."

Seppo's eyes rose to the dark night sky above as if seeking an answer there. "I do not know," he said at last. "I am…confused. I still recall my life as Talus in fragments. I have felt more…alive in recent months than ever before since Soot woke me all those years ago on Palantis."

"Do you remember what it was like to be human?" Eva asked. As soon as the words left her mouth, she regretted them.

Seppo let out a sigh and his metallic voice held a note of sadness and longing. "The things I remember are strange: the feel of the sun on my face, water running through my hands, grass beneath my feet, the touch of a loved one — I may be protected from age, disease, and weapons in this shell, but I have come to learn that it keeps out more than it lets in."

Eva reached up and wrapped her hand around one of Seppo's

fingers. "I'm sorry," she said, throat tight. "When you put it that way, it sounds like a terrible thing."

"Once, long, long ago, I thought this was the greatest thing I could ever do for my people," Seppo said. "Immortality! In my pride and vanity, I thought I would make us like the gods of Palantis. I thought I was a god — fashioning life eternal, cheating death and pain. How foolish I was."

Silence fell between them, broken only by the faint chirp of crickets. Eva looked at Tahl and the others.

"It doesn't sound like such a bad thing to want to keep the ones you love safe and with you forever," she said.

"Ah, mistress Evelyn," Seppo sighed. He bent down and, with surprising tenderness, plucked a budding wildflower from the edge of a rock at his feet. He held the new plant before him, bathing the delicate, half-grown petals in the light of his sapphire eyes.

"Love, happiness, joy — all the wonderful things of life are treasured because they do not last. Time may decay, but it also heightens, that most dear to us. When time is defeated, when moments such as those are infinite, they lose all meaning."

The golem fell silent, leaving Eva alone with her thoughts. Eventually, he reached down and nudged her back toward the rest, who were still sound asleep.

"You had better get some rest, mistress Evelyn," Seppo said. "We still have many miles to go."

Eva started back toward her spot next to Tahl then paused. "Seppo?"

"Yes?"

"I love you. Thank you, for everything."

The golem's blue eyes flared brighter for a moment and he gave a brief nod. Although his helmeted head could show no expression, it sounded to Eva like Seppo was smiling when he replied.

"You are most welcome."

The next few days were spent wandering and retracing their tracks, up rocky heights where the snow held firm and down into mist-covered valleys. The clouds rolled in and fog settled over everything until they couldn't even fly the gryphons clear of the haze. Unable to fly for more than a few hours, Carroc stumbled along on the ground with them, making the going even slower. At last, after four days of wandering, Soot threw down his cap in disgust.

"I can't make heads or tails of anything in this sky-cursed soup!"

Eva could tell he was angry at himself for letting them down and thus irritable overall. "We're going to have to wait it out, or I'm apt to lead us right off the edge of a cliff. We could be headed north into the Endless or straight south to the Ice Mountains for all I know."

They hunkered down in a valley by a river, each snapping at one another with nothing to do but dwell on their thoughts and succumb to boredom and irritation. When at last the sun shone clear, and they could fly the gryphons out of the forest canopy and valley, Eva had never been gladder to be in the sky.

Once again, she marveled at the glorious sights flying brought. Never ending, forest-coated mountains stretched in every direction, cut here and there by the river they'd been camped by as it wound its way to the east. Soaring through the clear blue skies, Eva took a moment to close her eyes and soak in the pale sunlight, glad to be free of the dreary gray smog. Even Carroc seemed to find renewed strength in his injured wing — Eva heard Tahl let loose a shout of joy and his white gryphon stretched his wings. He was almost back to normal thanks to Ivan's diligent care.

When they landed and reported what they'd seen to Soot, he clapped a hand to his head.

"Of course — what a windblown idiot I am!" he said. "We followed this river on the expedition — if we keep on going, it should open into a lake surrounded by cliffs. The low country is less than a week's travel away, on the other side of that lake."

Sure enough, it wasn't long before they spotted twin gray peaks split down the middle by a river gorge. The entire mountain chain rose so high that the tops were obscured by lofty, white clouds. As they drew closer, the canyon walls grew narrower and narrower, until they were forced to go single file on a footpath cut by wildlife down one side of the gorge. The roar of the water echoed on the rocks loud enough that they had to shout to be heard over its rushing waters. Eva glanced over the side and saw a raging current, hurtling trees limbs and chunks of ice smashing into the rock walls. From their vantage, it was a straight fall down, hundreds of feet to the turbulent river below.

"I think I'll fly over," Wynn said, peering down into the canyon below.

Soot shook his head. "Not a good idea. Last time we came through, Uthred almost got thrown off his gryphon trying." The smith pointed a gnarled finger up at the mountain peaks far, far above. "Canyon's too narrow to fly through and the winds up there are storming wicked — the gryphons'll have a rough enough go getting over on their own without the extra weight."

Eva looked at Tahl and saw concern for Carroc heavy on his face. But Soot refused to be swayed and they set about removing as much gear from the gryphons as they could carry. When they finished, Eva looked Fury in the eyes. "I know you — don't be showing off up there and get hurt."

The red gryphon rolled his head in a show of exasperation. Eva jerked on one of his lines to show she meant business. "I mean it, *be careful*. And take care of Carroc."

Fury bobbed his head and Eva threw her arms around his neck in a tight hug. Like usual, Fury twisted in her grip but Eva held on until he relaxed and wrapped his beak around her shoulder to return the gesture.

"See you on the other side," she said.

They waited for the gryphons to take flight. As Fury and the others grew smaller and smaller, Eva couldn't help but notice the tug of a breeze. She reached out and gave Tahl's hand a reassuring squeeze before turning to the canyon.

Seppo led the way. Although he technically had no reason to fear falling, his width forced him to edge along sideways, arms extended against the wall of the gorge. The rest followed close behind, Soot behind the golem. Chel brought up the rear, clutching the wall much the same as Seppo, although she had ample room to walk normally.

"What do you suppose we do if the trail ends?" Wynn asked, yelling to be heard over the crashing river. The wind had also increased in the tunnel and tugged at Eva's hair. She didn't want to think what it might be like up near the mountain peaks.

Eva glanced back and saw the look of terror on Chel's face and shook her head at Wynn. She wished she could make her way back to give the other girl some comfort and encouragement, but there was no way past the line of people between them. Instead, she motioned to Sigrid to offer her adopted sister some comfort.

"Don't worry — the fall alone would probably kill you," Sigrid yelled over the wind and water.

It didn't seem possible, but Chel's eyes grew even wider. Eva shot Sigrid a reproachful look. Rolling her eyes, Sigrid grabbed Chel's arm and gave her a gentle tug.

"Come on, I've got you."

As they continued in a long, slow procession, one careful step after the other, Eva realized the trail was narrowing. Eventually, Seppo had to press himself against the rock, sending occasional showers of pebbles down into the gorge whenever his heavy iron feet stepped on the edge. Even the humans turned sideways, and Eva found it hard to imagine flying through rough winds could have been worse than their current predicament.

A few yards later, the rock wall and the pathway grew slick with water. Craning her head up, Eva saw snowmelt trickling down the sheer cliff above. The thin path grew treacherous and their progress slowed by half. Eva worried about Chel, but there was no way to see back through the line of people to tell how she fared.

The sound of clattering rock froze them in place. Eva twisted around to look up, but Soot grabbed her arm and yanked her down into a squat.

"Don't look up, cover your head!"

Sure enough, a small slide of pebbles and fist-sized rocks rained down on them, the larger ones bouncing off the cliff far enough above to shoot out over them into the empty air above the river. They waited several moments until they were sure the slide had stopped before rising again.

An angry, shrieking wind picked up, ripping down the canyon and threatening to pry them from the cliff. Seppo managed to block the worst of it, but a couple of strong gusts left Eva clutching whatever handhold in the rocks she could find with her numb fingers. Eva shivered from the cold gusts, back soaked from the melting snow running down the back of the cliff. The sky above was nothing more than a narrow slit between the looming rock walls.

Morning turned into afternoon with no end in sight. At last, when Eva feared the path would end altogether and they would be forced to backtrack and find another route, they made a long sweeping turn to the north and caught a glimpse of an ice-covered lake.

"We're almost there now!" Soot yelled over the howling wind. "About a hundred more paces and the path widens!"

A crack of thunder burst above them.

"Duck!" Eva yelled. She crouched down as far as she could, cowering beneath her arms as snow, rock, and ice chunks cascaded down. The thunderous roar grew, accompanied by waves of heavy, wet snow — an avalanche. Just when Eva thought they would be swept away or buried, however, the slide began to slow.

Someone screamed behind Eva and her stomach seized in hot panic.

"Chel fell off the path!" Sigrid shouted. "I can't reach her!"

Eva shook the snow off her head and wiped her face, heart hammering. From her vantage, she could just see Chel clutching the cliff edge a few feet below the path where she'd been knocked down by the snow and debris.

Without a word, Seppo twisted around so his back was to the to the gorge and dropped off the ledge. He used his hands to pull himself toward Chel while Sigrid stretched out in a useless attempt to reach her.

Halfway to Chel, the rock path crumbled underneath his iron grip and Seppo slipped. Eva gasped. Showing surprising nimbleness, Seppo found a toehold and continued along. Although he'd covered half the distance, Eva still felt like Seppo was forever away. The wind shifted, and hungry, invisible hands tore at Chel.

"She's slipping!" Sigrid screamed in panic.

"Ivan, can't you do something?" Eva yelled over the roaring river and howling gusts.

The Scrawl shook his head. "I'd be just as likely to knock her off as help!"

With Seppo still an arm's length away, Chel's fingers finally lost purchase on the slick, jagged rock. She fell.

Roaring, Seppo vaulted from his foothold on the cliff and snagged Chel's wrist as she plummeted down to the river. Stretching out his hand, the golem clawed and dug into the crumbling cliff until he stopped sliding a short distance below the path but even farther out of reach than before.

As the rock gave way beneath his vice-like grip, Seppo swung a screaming Chel like a pendulum. Eva stretched out as far as she could and Soot wrapped himself around her legs, allowing her to descend another couple of feet.

Seppo swung again and released.

Chel shot up into the empty air like she'd been launched from a catapult.

Eva stretched with all her might.

Their arms grasped for one another.

For a brief instant, Eva feared Chel's added weight would tug her from Soot's hold. Instead, she felt them rising, her muscles screaming in protest at being stretched in two different directions. Roaring, Soot hauled them up to where Tahl could help pull them the rest of the way to safety.

Both women sobbed, chests heaving. When Eva opened her eyes and looked down, Seppo was nowhere to be seen.

Chapter 19

They rushed as fast as possible down the remainder of the path. Down below, the gorge opened up into the frozen lake and the steep, rock path widened into a long, sloping hillside. Eva sprinted down followed closely by the others. Reaching the inlet, she stopped at the edge of the rotted ice, where the roaring river met the lake. No sign of Seppo could be seen.

The gryphons met up with them shortly after. As relieved as Eva was to find them all safe and sound, she couldn't stop thinking about Seppo. After a short rest, the Windsworn took to the skies above the gorge, searching for the golem while the others made camp.

Eva tried to tell herself Seppo would be fine, that he couldn't drown and couldn't break so the fall wouldn't have killed him. But looking at the raging current, she imagined the golem stuck against a boulder beneath the water, the strength of the river pinning him in place. If that were the case it would be weeks — months, maybe — before the snow-fed river slowed enough for Seppo to fight free. Or, what if the current had pushed him all the way into the lake, under the ice?

Even if no one wanted to admit it, Seppo might be lost forever — their friend and their only chance of defeating the Smelterborn, too.

"It is all my fault," Chel said, tears streaking her face. "If I had not fell —"

"Better the bucket head than you," Soot said and then looked at the rest of them. "Seppo will be fine, you'll see. We'll make camp here on the lake shore and wait. He'll turn up."

But the way he said it, Eva wasn't sure if the smith was trying to reassure them or himself. Although it was a good spot to make camp — the best they'd had for days, — and the weather remained fair and warm, Eva couldn't help but feel like they'd lost the golem for good.

By nightfall, Seppo still hadn't returned. A somber mood fell over them, darker than any since the Battle of the Talon. Trying to get her mind off Seppo, Eva wondered what was going on back in Rhylance. She held out hope that the Smelterborn had been forced to retreat before they reached the Gryfonesse.

They felt Seppo's loss even more acutely when it came time to post watch. Saying he wasn't tired, Soot volunteered for the first shift, situating himself in sight of the gorge. Eva's heart went out to him — no matter how much the smith cursed and belittled Seppo, she knew he and the golem were the oldest and best of friends.

Before retiring, Eva excused herself from the rest and sat down in the loose pebbles on the beach beside her foster father.

"He'll make it," Soot said before Eva could speak. "You'll see."

"We'll wait for him," Eva promised. "We didn't come all this way to let a little water beat us."

For a while, neither of them said anything, thoughts drowned out by the rushing river.

"What I wouldn't give to be back at my forge," Soot said at last. "When this is all over, a whole army of Smelterborn won't be able to drag me out of it. I'm thinking about starting a garden in the back, by the stables."

Eva nodded. "That sounds nice."

"What about you, miss?" he asked. Soot jerked his head back at Tahl and the rest of camp. "Has the new queen found herself a king?"

Eva blushed and stammered, but Soot held up a hand. "The first time I met that kid, I was awful tempted to put a dent in his pretty face with my hammer," he said. "But now, I can't think of a better man to be by your side. I have a hunch your uncles — and father — would approve of him too."

"Really?" Eva said a smile spread across her face.

"Really."

Overcome with emotion and love for the old smith, Eva flung herself around Soot's thick neck and buried her face in his burly chest . Soot returned the embrace and gave her a reassuring pat on the back.

"I don't know what I'd do without you," Eva whispered into his hairy ear.

"Hey now, don't go getting all soft on me." Eva pulled back and caught Soot, wiping a tear from his eye. "You're going to melt through my old iron heart."

Eva laughed and then a splashing sound caused them both to peer into the darkness toward the river. Gravel crunched under iron boots and a large shadow loomed closer. Moments later, two bright blue eyes shone through the darkness toward them.

"Are you *crying*, Master Wayland?" Seppo's metallic voice rang out in the night, incredulous.

"Am not," Soot said, sniffing and wiping the back of his hand across his nose. "About time you showed up, I was just about to have to take your watch for you, you old rust bucket."

"Seppo!" Eva yelled. She jumped to her feet and ran to meet the golem wrapping herself around his cold, wet, armored waist.

"I do not want to do that again," Seppo said in a flat voice. "Please be more careful next time."

Morning dawned bright and sunny, enlightening the cheer surrounding Seppo's return. Foraging, Chel and Wynn managed to find some fresh tubers. Ivan used a bit of fancy rune magic to melt a hole through the ice and catch fresh fish. After short rations for days, the group gorged on the food, grateful for something besides old, dried provisions from the Scrawls and scrawny deer, elk or rabbit.

After they were all well fed, Soot gathered them around again and drew another map in the dark sand along the lakeshore.

"There's only one way out of the eastern end of the valley," he said, drawing a crude representation with his finger. "From there, it's pretty straightforward. We follow the river through the eastern woodlands, all the way down to the sea. Move north along the coast until we see Palantis."

"Well, that doesn't sound so bad!" Wynn said.

Soot raised his bushy eyebrows. "The woodlands are probably crawling with Smelterborn. The army might have even beaten us back. The Endless Plains are pretty much a straight shot across Altaris and even though the clankers are slow, they don't rest. What's more, there's not much game in the woodlands — at least there wasn't when we passed through and I doubt things have improved any."

"That's all, huh?" Sigrid said. "You make it sound like a walk through a field of wildflowers!"

Soot shared a look with Seppo. "You neglected to mention the Runefolk," the golem said in a cheerful voice.

Everyone else shared a confused glance. "What are …Runefolk?" Chel asked.

Soot scowled. "Nasty little people. We ran into them several times on our first journey. As far as we could guess, they're either the descendants of Palantine slaves or descendants of the Palantines themselves. Not every impressive offspring, either way. They're more like little weasels than humans."

"They pose no threat individually," Seppo said. "Which is why they wait until your back is turned or they outnumber you five to one before attacking."

Eva held back a long sigh. "Anything else we need to know about? Rivers of lava? Pestilence?"

Soot got the sarcasm but Seppo tapped a finger to his chin, apparently deep in thought. "No," he said at last. "I think that is all. Until we get to Palantis, of course. Who knows what new dangers await us there?"

"Fantastic," Wynn muttered, echoing the rest of the group's feelings.

They packed up camp and the gryphon riders took to the sky,

hoping to scout a path around the lake shore and out the other end of the lake valley. Reaching the eastern side, however, the beach ended abruptly. Flying over the lake's outlet, they found the path heading east had collapsed from the cliffside. Sheer rock rose all the way around inside the caldera meaning the only way out would be by flight…or swimming.

"No," Seppo said, folding his arms across his chest plate. "I am already rusting from my last trip underwater."

"Oh you'll be fine," Soot said. "A little more water isn't going to hurt you. But if you've got another suggestion as to how we're going to get your iron ass out of here, I'd love to hear it."

"I…" Seppo raised a hopeful finger and then sighed, shoulders drooping. "Fine."

They all lined up on the shore to bid him farewell.

"You humans don't understand what it is like down there," the golem whined. "Like walking through tar — I sink up to my knees in that mud. And the fish! They try to swim inside my helmet. My armor fills up with water, it's like trying to walk in a big wet coat while carrying two buckets."

"Good thing you're a wonder of ancient craftsmanship," Eva said, trying to appeal to the golem's pride. "If you weren't so well put together it might be a real problem."

"Hmph," Seppo pouted. "Let's just get it over with."

They mounted the gryphons in short order: Chel with Eva, Soot with Wynn and Ivan with Sigrid to give Carroc a lighter load carrying just Tahl. As they rose into the air, they waved down at Seppo, who watched them go.

"Hold up," Soot yelled once they were all in the sky. "I want to see how the big pile of slag does this."

At first, Seppo tried to pick his way around the base of the cliff. He made it a stone's throw from the beach before running out of hand and foot holds which forced him to retreat back to where he'd started. Next, Seppo tried to find a place where the ice around the shore wasn't rotten. He stretched forth a toe forward like a cat testing a puddle. When that proved impossible, he raised a hand and, shaking a fist at them, waded out into the water. When he reached the edge of the solid ice, Eva was surprised to find it thick enough for the golem to crawl on top of. After bouncing a few times to test its strength, Seppo strode across the lake, eager to reach the narrow chasm where the lake spilled out into the woodlands beyond the caldera.

He made it almost two-thirds of the way across when the ice cracked and he sank to the waist. Seppo flailed, trying to pull himself back onto the stable ice, but the cracks spread. Moments, later he was completely submerged to his torso. He shook his fist at them again and shouted something Eva couldn't hear. They shared a chuckle, which turned into an outright laugh, as the chunk of ice Seppo leaned on broke and he sank below the surface. After a few moments, it was clear the golem wouldn't resurface.

"Come on," Soot said. "He'll be fine. No sense waiting around here."

With a last look at the hole in the ice, Eva turned Fury eastward and they soared over the peaks of the mountains. For whatever reason, the winds proved to be much gentler on the eastern side of the rock rim. When they reached the peaks, a flurry of white puffs bounded across a narrow precipice. Fury's head followed the mountain sheep and he dipped lower.

"You can come back and get dinner later," Eva said, pulling up on the reins. As the shadows of the gryphons passed overhead, the animals scattered with incredible speed across the smallest of footholds.

On the other side of the mountains, just as Soot said it would, the land opened up into a wide park. After a steep drop through some rocks that would surely cause Seppo even more complaint, the river cut through open meadows fringed with trees. At the lower elevation, Eva saw many of the aspens and cottonwoods covered in small leaves — a sign of high spring.

She gazed off to the east, following the line of the river, before it disappeared into heavier woodlands, eventually winding out of sight behind a series of rolling hills miles and miles away. They landed on the banks of the river in grass already above their ankles. With plenty of food from the morning fishing, and young greens scavenged across the meadow, they made a quick sweep of the immediate area then returned to set up camp. With nothing to do but wait for Seppo, everyone relaxed for the first time in ages. The gryphons played, scrapping on the ground like overgrown kittens before shooting into the air to dip and twist at each other in mock battle. Soot propped himself up against a boulder and promptly fell asleep in the sunshine.

"How about a little walk?" Tahl asked Eva while the others each found various forms of entertainment.

"Are you asking to court me, sir?" Eva said in mock formality.

Tahl grinned and extended a hand. "Why yes, fair maiden. Tis too beautiful a day to pass without a stroll along yonder river."

Laughing, Eva held out her hands. Tahl pulled her to her feet and they walked away from the others, trying not to draw too much attention to themselves. Passing by Soot, one of the smith's eyes cracked open.

"Hey, you two lovebirds, stay within shouting range," he muttered. "Just because the sun is shining and the birds are singing doesn't mean it's safe to start frittering around with spring fever."

Eva rolled her eyes but promised they would. Then, unable to restrain herself any longer, she shot off, running through the new grass. She didn't stop until she passed beyond a stand of bushes, hiding them from the sight of the others. Tahl tackled her to the ground as soon as she stopped. They rolled in a tumble and ended up on their backs, laughing and gasping for air.

As soon as he'd caught his breath, Tahl leaned over and placed a long kiss on Eva's lips.

"That's better," he said when they pulled apart at last. They'd hardly found any private time in the last few months.

"We shouldn't stay long," Eva said after she kissed him again.

Tahl put up a finger to her lips. "I'm going to pretend I didn't hear that."

Soot's shouts recalled them back to camp sometime later and they came around the bend just in time to see Seppo sloshing out of the river. His dull iron plates were splattered with dark river mud that stuck to the golem like tar. Muttering, he peeled away as much of it as he could, disgust plain in his voice.

"Never. Again," the golem said after emerging from the river free of mud. The sun soon wicked the water from his armored plates. Seeing them all trying to hide their laughter only soured his mood further. "I'm sure it's all very funny to you. You've been lounging around here for hours while I slogged away through the muck and sand and river to get here. I'll never get it all out of my joints."

"It's alright, big fella," Ivan said, holding out a handful of young tubers. "We saved you something to eat?"

In a flash, Seppo swooped the Scrawl up in his arms and hoisted Ivan over his head.

"Put me down you storming golem!" Ivan shouted, flailing and kicking. As Seppo neared a small eddy carved out from the river he struggled even harder — to no avail.

"You wouldn't dare — you don't even get wet! Put me — AGH!"

Shrugging his shoulders, Seppo tossed Ivan into the frigid water. The Scrawl came up moments later, spluttering and shivering. The rest roared with laughter.

"I don't see what's so funny," Ivan said. He snapped his fingers to heat his body, sending a wave of steam rising from his clothes. "I'll be lucky if I don't get a cough and die out here in the middle of nowhere."

Although there were still quite a few hours of daylight left, they agreed to stay overnight at their current camp. As evening faded, thousands of stars streamed down overhead among a sky of deep purples and blues. They reclined back, staring into the fathomless beyond.

"The Juarag have a legend," Chel said breaking the silence and surprising them all. She usually kept to herself, especially since the incident in the gorge. "Our shamans say that the Earth Father fell in love with Lady Night. He waited each day for the sun to rest, for the darkness to fall and the moon to rise. But no matter how hard he tried, he could never get the attention of Lady Night, for she was given to much mischief and trickery and toyed with his affections. After many years, Father Earth grew desperate for her love. In a last attempt to win over Lady Night, he scooped out the precious stones of the earth and flung them into the sky."

"What did she do?" Eva asked, pulling Tahl's arms tighter around her as she reclined in his lap, listening to Chel's story.

"Lady Night was indeed pleased with the gift, but before she could confess her feelings, Grandfather Sun rose again in the east and chased her from the skies. She had waited too long. It is said when you see a star falling from the sky, that is Lady Night weeping, returning one of Fathers Earth's precious stones to him, for she feels unworthy of such a great gift."

Sigrid snorted and rolled over but Eva saw Wynn stare up into the night, mouth open. "What a beautiful story," the younger girl said in a hushed voice.

Before Sigrid could come up with some snide retort, Eva looked at Ivan, who was sitting to her left. "Now that you're dried off, how about a story, master Scrawl?" she said.

Ivan sniffed. "Huh."

"Oh come on, Ivan," Tahl said. "Don't be that way!"

"Fine, fine," Ivan said. He thought for a moment and then a smile spread across his face. "There was once a golem —"

"Oh, I like this one," Seppo said, blue eyes shining across the fire.

"— there was once a golem who picked on folk smaller than himself and threw them into rivers —"

"Ivan!" they shouted in unison.

The Scrawl held up his hands as Seppo began to rise. "Fine, fine. A real story. What do you want to hear about?"

"A great battle," Sigrid said.

"A golem!" Seppo said.

From outside the fire ring, Fury raised his head and let out a kree, signaling he wanted a tale about gryphons. The other gryphons added their calls to his.

"How about a story that'll put you noisy bunch to sleep?" Soot huffed, his doze interrupted by the sudden ruckus.

Ivan tapped his finger on his tattooed chin for a long moment. "Alright, I've got one. This is the tale of Eleanor, the first Queen of the Windsworn," he looked over at Fury. "And there's gryphons in it, I promise."

"You mean the Queen of Rhylance?" Eva said. "The Windsworn don't have a queen, they have a commander."

Ivan shook his head. "According to our records, in the first days the Sorondarans came to Altaris, their kings and queen ruled over both the people and the gryphon riders. It was only in the last few generations that the title was split.

"Eleanor was the only surviving daughter of the King and Queen of Sorondar. Her mother was killed in the great plague that caused the Sorondarans to flee their homeland and sail east. Soon after she landed upon Altaris, her father passed away as well, overcome by grief. Forced to lead her people in a strange new land at a young age, Eleanor didn't know what to do or where to turn to.

"The Sorondarans made their camps on the beach for a time. Although there were little resources for shelter and they didn't have much to eat, they feared a journey farther inland would be too hard on the gryphon eggs. None of the gryphons from Sorondar had been put on the ship, for the disease hit them even harder than it did the humans. The people hoped the eggs would hatch free of the sickness. There were less than two score in all, carefully tended all the way across the ocean."

"Did they make it?" Wynn asked, even more enamored with Ivan's story than she had been with Chel's.

Sigrid tapped her on the back of the head. "Think about it! How else would there be gryphons if they hadn't?"

Wynn's face flushed and she fell silent, allowing Ivan to continue.

"As queen, Eleanor was the first to participate in the Choosing when the hatching time came. She carefully held each one, waiting for a sign that the egg was hatching, that the gryphon inside had chosen her. But each time, the egg remained still. At first, the Sorondarans feared the egg-chicks had not survived the journey, but behind the queen came others, and the eggs hatched for them.

"As Eleanor passed from egg to egg and reached the last few, the Sorondarans began to mutter among themselves. How could they be led by a girl who was not chosen by the gryphons? The eggs continued to tick down, one by one, until Eleanor came to the last one."

Ivan paused and looked at Eva. "What color of egg do you suppose it was?"

She'd never heard the story before but Eva had a pretty good idea what the answer was. "Red?"

The Scrawl nodded. "It was the first blood egg — the only one of that line brought over across the ocean. Since then, the line of blood gryphons is a straight one, all the way down to Fury here." He turned and gestured to Fury, who stretched his neck out and held his head high.

"What about Eleanor?" Wynn asked. "What happened next?"

"According to the legends, when her hatchling had grown large enough to carry her, she began to fly east, in search of a home for her people. They had lived along the coast for the first year and the winter hit them hard. Even with the help of the Scrawls, they did not fare well. Neither did the gryphons thrive in the coastland — they were made for mountains.

"Flying east, it is said Eleanor caught sight of the Gyr just before sunset, the last light of the day illuminating the mighty mountain. She flew all night toward the mountain until morning came and revealed it once more. The stories say she landed on the Gyr's peak and declared the Sorondarans and their gryphons would never have another home. There are many stories that followed, of how Eleanor settled the Rhylance valley for her people and led them through famine, storms and even civil war to lay the foundations for your people today. She also trained the first generation of new gryphon riders. Although she was young and felt unready to assume the throne, she overcame all odds to be known as one of the greatest rulers in the history of your people."

As he finished, Ivan looked Eva in the eyes and she glanced away while the others broke into applause. Wrapped in her thoughts, she hardly noticed when Ivan started singing a beautiful, haunting song about a Scrawl returning home to his beloved. Listening to the strange words washed away Eva's anxiety and she looked around the fire, smiling. For the time being, at least, her loved ones were warm, happy and safe.

This, she thought, *this is what we're fighting for.*

Chapter

20

Days later, signs of the ancient Palantines appeared along the river: ancient, toppled buildings covered in vines, bits and pieces of roads blanketed with moss and grass, and patches of clearings overgrown by wildflowers — all that remained, Seppo said, of once-fertile farmlands. Although Soot warned them to stay on guard, it was impossible not to enjoy the fair weather in the woodlands.

Not long past the feral farmlands, they spotted a small villa sitting atop a grass-covered knoll. The ruins stood watch above a stretch of overgrown fields divided by cracked and fallen stone fences. After flying ahead, Sigrid and Wynn reported the surrounding area devoid of Runefolk or animals. They met together at the top of the hill to survey the surrounding countryside with Seppo.

"This is incredible!" Ivan said. His eyes flitted from one collapsed building to another. Many were two stories high, including what looked to have once been a granary, half of its dome caved in and leaning across the remnants of the building next to it. On the other end of town, a lone tower about three stories high still stood, the dilapidated roof revealing a large tarnished bell at the top. Before they could stop him, Ivan wandered off, poking his head from building to building.

Eva noticed many of the buildings, as rundown as they were,

looked very similar to those in the older parts of Gryfonesse. When she pointed this out to Soot, he nodded.

"Gryfonesse was built on top of an old Palantine city. Many of the buildings, including the citadel and parts of the outer walls, were just repaired, strengthened and expanded."

While they were talking, the others started exploring what was left of structures.

"Not much left," Tahl said, coming out of what looked like a small cottage. There's a few rusted tools and things, but they're far beyond use. Everything else has rotted away."

"We should keep moving," Soot said, scanning the surrounding lands below the villa. "We're too exposed up here — I don't like it."

Eva followed his gaze. In many areas, the woods encroached on the old fields, providing plenty of cover for ambush. In the distance, a glint of silver marked the river, still winding its easy path east between hills and trees. She hadn't realized how far they'd strayed from it until now.

"I agree," Eva said. "We shouldn't stay here."

Gathering the others, she found Ivan last, climbing over a large foundation with only one wall remaining. On the inside, Eva saw a number of runes carved into a large mosaic. The paint was faded and chipped, but she could still make out most of the mural: it showed a series of white-robed people, holding out offerings to a woman clothed in flame, descending from the sun.

"One of the ancient Palantine gods," Ivan said, stepping close enough to run a hand over the cracked tiles. "The Sun Mother — goddess of fields and the summer. I can't believe it!"

The Scrawl knelt down below the picture to examine the runes. As he traced over each one, his lips moved in silence. When he'd finished the first line, Eva saw Ivan's face go pale and he jerked his hand back as if he'd been burned by the stone.

"What is it?" Eva asked. "What does it say?"

"It is a sacrificial altar," Seppo said. Eva jumped. She hadn't heard the golem approach. "My people practiced blood sacrifice — our gods were never sated. We should leave this place."

Seppo's sudden, somber mood change made Eva nervous. She figured this must be the memories of Talus flooding to the forefront again and needed no further encouragement to get them moving again.

"Let's go!" Eva shouted, whistling for Fury. "Time to —"

A loud clanging sounded from the tower. Spinning to see the cause of the nose, Eva caught sight of Wynn leaping from the second floor of the bell tower. The ancient bell peeled, the mournful song reverberating across the countryside. A moment later, its beam broke and crashed down. Whirls of dust rose from the skeleton of the tower as Eva rushed forward to help Wynn to her feet after the long fall.

"What in the sky were you thinking?" Eva hissed after making sure the younger girl was okay.

"I…I just wanted to see if it worked is all!" Wynn said, "There was a chain — I didn't think it would hurt to give it a tug."

"You storming idiot!" Sigrid yelled. "Next time do us all a favor and let the bell smash you!"

Eva turned to tell Sigrid to let it go, but Fury and then other gryphons interrupted her, letting out a warning call overhead. Falling back on their training, Tahl and Sigrid leaped on the back of their gryphons as soon as they landed.

"We've got company!" Tahl yelled once they'd taken off again.

"What is it?" Soot asked, shading his eyes to look up at them.

"Looks like a pack of those Runefolks you were talking about," Sigrid said. Her voice gave no sign of panic, just mild interest. "Scrawny little things, anyway. We must have done something to tick them off, though — they're coming out of the forest from everywhere."

"This will be a sacred site to them, given the altar," Seppo said. "It is time for us to depart!"

Loading everyone but Seppo on the gryphons, they took off. Just as Sigrid and Tahl reported, dozens of skinny men and women poured out of the trees about a quarter-mile away. Their hair was matted and wild, their clothes little more than raw hides stitched together. They were armed with rusted, ancient weapons: spears, crude bows, clubs, and hatchets. Eva didn't need to see more.

"Let's go!" she shouted, as Fury banked away toward the river, wings surging. Chel held on tight behind her.

With Seppo at a full run below them, they pushed the gryphons to their limit. Looking back, Eva saw the Runefolk stop atop the hill, screaming some broken language and shaking their weapons. Thankfully, they didn't give pursuit. Even so, Eva kept flying until almost nightfall before making camp on a small island in the middle of the river — the safest place they could find.

As they made a meager, cold camp, Wynn remained silent, ignored by the rest of the party as they went about their different duties and assignments. While the others were preoccupied, Eva pulled her aside and saw the girl twist away to wipe her eyes.

"I know, I know," Wynn said in a dull voice. "I'm a storming idiot."

"There's no harm done," Eva said, "but I hope you learned an important lesson today. What one of us does can affect the entire group. Do you understand?"

Wynn nodded and Eva pulled her into a hug. "I'm sorry," the girl sniffed. "I'll do better."

"I know you will," Eva replied, patting her on the back. "We're all going to have to be on our guard, especially now."

On edge from the day's events, it took a long time for the group to fall asleep, even with the added comfort of knowing they were protected by the river and had Seppo watching over them. Without a fire, the camp felt dreary, even though the night proved to be mild. It took Eva a long time to finally drift off to sleep.

"*Attack! Attack!*"

Sigrid's shouts cut through the night, immediately rousing everyone. Eva shot to her feet, trying to pull her sword free and untangle herself from Fury, Tahl and her cloak. It was the gray hour before dawn, but she still spotted several shapes surging toward them from the opposite end of the narrow island.

The others came to their feet, cursing and reaching for their weapons. Eva heard Seppo's yell and saw a flash of the golem's blue eyes as he threw himself at the Runefolk, throwing them aside like straw dolls. Hearing shouting behind her, Eva spun to find a man running toward her, his crude spear leveled at her chest. With no time for the fear to set in, she knocked the spearhead aside and killed the unarmored man with a single cut of her sword as he stumbled forward from his missed stab.

"They're coming from all sides!" she shouted.

Not waiting for the next opponent to find her, Eva ran to the bank, hacking through two more Runefolk on the way. Yelling again, Eva tried to rally the others around her, using the intermittent flashes of light from Ivan's rune fire to spot them.

Wynn and Chel joined her while Tahl and Soot stood together, cutting through more of the Runefolk as they leaped into the shallows from crudely-fashioned rafts. Behind them, the gryphons tore through another landing party, talons, and beaks making short work of the unarmored people.

Half-submerged in the river, several Runefolk crawled over Seppo like ants, screaming and beating at his armor with their poor weaponry to no avail. Reaching back, he threw two into the swift current. Ignoring those still clinging to him, Seppo waded to another raft and pummeled it to pieces with his fists. Eva, Chel, and Wynn ran to help Soot and Tahl. As soon as they arrived and cut down a couple more of the Runefolk, however, the savages retreated to their remaining rafts, the fight gone from them.

"Get outta here!" Sigrid snarled, slashing at the water with her ax.

Back on the shore, Seppo picked up the Runefolk's dead bodies and unceremoniously dumped them in the river. Eva studied one of the men she'd killed. He had a ragged beard over a face spotted with sores. Crude rune markings had been painted on his face with what looked like blood. As revolted as she was, Eva couldn't help but pity the primitive people — by the looks of it, they led a hard, unforgiving life. Once again, she felt an immense relief when everyone reported no serious injury.

"What in the blazes was that?" Soot asked. "Can't have been the same ones that we saw back at the town — there's no way they could have traveled that fast."

"They must have seen us land," Tahl replied, wiping a streak of blood from his cheek.

"Huh," Sigrid said. "That's the last time I ever pee in the middle of the night alone again. Next time I'm waking you up to come with me, Wynn."

They all stared at her for a moment, everyone thinking the same thing but no one daring to ask. Finally, Eva — fighting to keep a straight face — spoke up. "You...you were?"

"Yeah, they caught me with my pants down, alright?" Sigrid snapped. "I told Seppo to look away, which is why he didn't see them. Almost got an arrow in my rear!"

Ivan snorted and, like the first trickle of water in a breaking dam, they all burst into wild laughter. Sigrid glowered and looked like she wanted nothing more than to punch one of them in the face.

"I don't see what's so funny," she said, voice and temper rising. "It could've happened to anyone one of you!"

"I — I'm surprised you didn't tell them to piss off!" Ivan gasped out. They roared again. Tears ran down Eva's face and she fought to calm herself, knowing Sigrid was only seconds away from pummeling someone into the ground.

"I hate to interrupt," Seppo said. "But it appears we have more company coming."

The laughter died right away. In the gray dawn, Eva looked to the north shore of the river. Dozens of orange eyes burned like the fires of some hellish furnace. No feral, diseased excuses for humans these. They could only be one thing: Smelterborn, and plenty of them.

Chapter
21

Storm it all," Soot said in a low voice. Eva turned around and found just as many Smelterborn waiting on the southern bank.

"The Runefolk were a diversion," Chel said, breaking the silence. "This is what was really waiting."

No one spoke as the Smelterborn filed out of the trees and lined both banks, close to fifty in all. They were an array of all makes — wide, heavy plated golems wielding enormous swords, maces and shields three men couldn't lift, lighter, taller scouts, with their long spears and Shadowstalkers, ebony armor soaking in the first rays of sun stretching through the trees.

"Any ideas, fearless leader?" Sigrid asked Eva. The humans and gryphons all drew toward the middle of the island and formed a half-circle, weapons drawn. The gryphons hissed and gouged the earth with their talons. Meanwhile, the Smelterborn just watched.

Eva could hardly believe they'd been laughing just minutes before. There certainly wasn't anything to laugh about now.

"We get in the sky as fast as we can," Eva said. "Seppo, you can outrun them, especially if we head downstream. We don't stop until we lose them, no matter what."

"No."

Seppo's voice cut through the silence as they prepared to break for the gryphons.

"No, what, you old bucket of rust?" Soot asked. "You got a better idea?"

The golem nodded. "You will run, I will stay. They are here for me."

Studying the collection of Smelterborn, Eva got the sinking feeling Seppo was right. The golems' flaming gaze seemed to track Seppo's every move, studying their prey.

"Seppo, no," Eva said. "We won't let them take you."

"You will find a way," Seppo said. "It is better to live and fight again than die here, especially for me. They will not kill me. Ogunn needs me — he knows it. You must flee before he reclaims the stones."

"We're not leaving you," Soot said, clutching the black stone in his hand. Red light pulsed between his fingers. "We're in this together, dammit. You may have started it all those years ago, but we're going to help you finish it. We're going to see it done."

Seppo shook his head. "Please, you must go now."

Instead, Eva hefted her sword higher, the runes on the blade glowing in the presence of so many Smelterborn. "We're with you," Eva said. "They're not taking you."

As if hearing Eva's words, the Smelterborn stepped off both banks, forming lines of five. Each step they took, the dirty water raged higher and higher passing by them like rocks in the current. Eva gave up her brief hope of the golem's being swept away. After four steps, heads of the front line disappeared beneath the water, with more still coming off the shoreline. Eva gripped her sword tight.

Behind Eva, Ivan's voice suddenly rose. In the midst of a kenning, he waved and twisted his arms and fingers, voice growing louder and louder. A rumble sounded and the water between them and the north bank began to spin, forming a whirlpool in the midst of the current. Various runes flared to life across Ivan's body as he invoked their names. Eva saw one Smelterborn tip over and wash away, followed by another.

Ivan shouted louder and louder. His whirlpool raged but the Smelterborn still came on. Seeing them overcome the effort, Eva shouted for the Scrawl to stop. "Save your strength! We're going to have to fight them!"

Seppo cracked his iron hands and swung his arms like a fighter limbering up. "Come on, slaves! Let us see if you can beat the First Golem!"

A Smelterborn's helmeted head rose out of the water a stone's throw from the island, followed by another. Roaring, the golem yanked the first Shadowstalker out of the river and hurled it downstream. Eva swung down on a Smelterborn just emerging from the water. Her sword cut through its head and the empty husk fell back as its spirit whipped by her. Without thinking Eva swung again, her rune sword slashing another's arm off as it stretched out for her. Seppo wrestled in water up to his hip with two other Smelterborn, smashing them together before ripping the head off one of his opponents.

"A little help!" Sigrid shouted. Eva found them overwhelmed. Ivan desperately held back three Smelterborn on his own while the others desperately fought the rest. With no rune magic or enchanted weapons to help them, they could do little but parry the blows and do their best not to be crushed beneath the Smelterborn's strokes.

A Smelterborn sliced through the air above Wynn's head with a giant ax. Eva stabbed up through its back plate and Tahl smashed into the golem with his shield. The golem crumpled, falling on top of another.

No matter how well they fought, the Smelterborn still gained ground. Working in eerie concert, the golems drove the companions to the eastern edge of the island. With the gryphons grounded beside them, there was hardly any room to maneuver. The banks dropped off on both sides, forming a small bottleneck that Seppo did his best to fill with Eva and Ivan supporting him.

The urge to wield her Wonder and drive the golems back gripped Eva. In the past, she'd used it to fight the Smelterborn with great effect, but Seppo had cautioned her not to reveal the stone now that they knew its connection to the First Forge. Now, it looked like it might be their only chance of escape.

"We can't hold!" Ivan shouted in between kennings. Even in the dim light, Eva could see dark rings under his eyes, in stark contrast to his paling face.

"Go!" Seppo yelled as he locked arms with yet another golem and hurled it into the deep water. "You must go before they get the stones!"

"We're not leaving you!" Eva yelled. "We're all getting out together!"

A pair of larger Smelterborn charged Seppo. The friendly golem met them head-on, his iron boots sliding backward in the sand as they bull rushed him and he fought to hold them back. While they were entangled, Eva cut through one, allowing Seppo to crush in the head of the other. The remaining Smelterborn paused, staring at them with burning eyes. Eva wasted no time.

"Everyone but Ivan get on the gryphons," Eva said. "Ivan, Seppo and I will hold them here."

"I'm not leaving you," Tahl said. Eva shook her head.

"There's not room for all of us down here," she said. "You can protect us more up there."

With one last look, Tahl swore and sprinted to Carroc. Sigrid, Wynn, and Chel mounted as well.

"I'm not going anywhere, missy."

Soot's voice settled a steady calm over Eva.

"They've got the numbers but we can hold," he said. He thumped his large two-handed maul on the ground. "Come on you damn clankers!"

The Smelterborn held fast. Tahl and the others hovered overhead, no one sure what to do.

Their ranks parted, revealing a Smelterborn unlike any Eva had ever seen before. His armor was a dull black, much like the stalkers, but covered in so many runes they looked like veins of fire running across its body. He stood leaner than the regular Smelterborn, but thicker than the scouts — much like, Eva realized…Seppo.

She recognized the new golem, although he was much smaller than in her dream back at the Talon. Eva sensed the lights of her Wonder fading in the black-armored golem's presence and felt the stone's reassuring warmth flicker and snuff out. A shudder ran through her as its deep red eyes burned across her before settling on Seppo.

"Well met, Talus," the new golem replied.

"Talus is dead," Seppo said. "He died centuries ago, in the First Forge, as his creations should have."

The golem flicked a hand away as if to toss Seppo's reply into the river. "Such are the thoughts of narrow-minded men. Nevertheless, here we are now: master and apprentice. I don't think I need to tell you I've been looking for you. Your work is incomplete, master. Much as I hate to admit it, my grand design cannot be finished without you."

"Some paths are better left untrod, Ilmaren," Seppo said. "Or shall I call you Ogunn?"

Ogunn/Ilmaren shrugged. "Nevertheless, it is up to great men such as us to go down them. And Ilmaren is as dead as Talus."

"Whatever notions of greatness I once had, I know them now to be false," Seppo said. "And whatever you are now, it is not a man."

Ogunn clenched his fists and smoke rose from his armor. "I have not spent years hunting for you to trade witty banter. I no longer require living souls to create life from the First Forge. I have surpassed your wildest dreams."

"You have made the First Forge into an abomination," Seppo said, voice tinged with sadness. "We were men, Ilmaren, not gods."

"Nevertheless," Ogunn said, waving a hand. "I think you already know my new Smelterborn are flawed — they cannot be away from the sustaining power of the First Forge long enough to complete the conquest of my empire. You will return with me to Palantis and help my glorious future come to pass."

Seppo shook his head. "I am afraid you are mistaken, Ilmaren. My memory was corrupted the first time I stopped your evil work. I no longer recall the secrets you desire."

Ogunn threw back his head and laughed an awful, booming sound. "We shall see." He pointed to Eva and Soot. "If what you say is true, I hope you remember for their sake. Otherwise, they will pay with their lives."

"You can't have him!" Eva shouted, filled with sudden courage. The Wonder stone glowed against her skin, so bright its golden, blue and pink lights burst through her tunic and chainmail.

Ogunn's eyes fell on her and Eva felt the courage burn out of her like a hot blade quenched in oil. "I know who you are, girl," the golem said, voice dropping to a low hiss. "You're the waif who destroyed my host — that pathetic woman, Celina. And it was you who aided the thief who stole the Deimos from me. You will pay for your impudence."

Soot growled, twisting his hand around his mattock. Ivan clenched his fists and they flared with a cold blue light. Both stepped forward as if to shield Eva.

"You will not harm them," Seppo said.

"I know the stones are here, both the Deimos and Aithos. They call to us — do you not feel it, master?" Ogunn's eyes flared and fire spat out of his helmet as he spoke. "I will have them…now!"

"Run, mistress Evelyn!" Seppo shouted.

The two golems collided.

Eva stumbled backward, staring at the titanic battle between Seppo and Ogunn. Unlike the other Smelterborn, Ogunn was an even match for Seppo, if not stronger. As the golems locked arms, a screech of clashing metal reverberated over the river.

"We can't help him now!" Soot yelled, pulling a struggling Eva toward Fury.

Eva continued to fight but couldn't break free of Soot's iron grip. Seppo and Ogunn exchanged hammer-like blows strong enough to fell a horse. While they pummeled one another unceasingly, the rest of the Smelterborn closed in on Eva, Soot, and Ivan.

Now other Smelterborn joined the fight against Seppo, raining blows down on his back and sides while he struggled to hold Ogunn at bay. One last wild punch from his former apprentice knocked Seppo to the ground.

"*No!*" As Fury landed, Eva wrenched free from Soot, rushing to Seppo.

Eva slashed through one scout with her rune blade and then

149

another, but the rest of the Smelterborn fell in a circle around Seppo and their master, an impenetrable wall of iron.

Eva turned just in time to see a Smelterborn swinging its shield at her. She attempted to parry with her sword but the blow launched her backward through the air and she landed hard on her back, gasping for air. Fury leaped and landed at Eva's side as Soot rushed forward, armed with only a hammer.

The smith struck the Smelterborn once. The golem used his shield to shed the blow like it was a child's toy. In the same motion, it swung its other arm in a backhand and Soot went flying into a motionless heap on the sand.

While Tahl rushed to drag the unconscious smith onto the back of Carroc, Ivan dispatched the golem with a blast of ice to the face. The exertion left him doubled over, completely drained.

Dazed, Eva lifted a hand to her forehead and her fingertips came away wet with blood. Her world spun as Wynn and Chel yelled at her to get on Fury. Next thing she knew, she was slumped over the saddle, Chel holding her in place.

Roaring, Ogunn pushed his way through the throng. Eva caught a brief glimpse of Seppo lying on the ground, alive, although he was held immobile beneath the weight of a dozen Smelterborn as the golems wrapped him in chains.

"*STOP THEM!*"

Ogunn lunged for Fury as the red gryphon rose into the air. Eva felt a jerk as the golem's hand wrapped around Fury's tail.

Like a bolt from a ballista, Sven struck at full speed. Fury screamed and pulled free, wings heaving to rise out of the golem's reach. As Sigrid and Sven crashed in a tangle with Ogunn, Eva's senses cleared.

"Sigrid, get out of there!" she screamed. She tried to urge Fury back to the fight but he refused.

Sven clawed and gouged at Ogunn with his talons and beak. Once free from her leg harness, Sigrid dropped down and drew both axes, hacking at the surrounding Smelterborn. Roaring like a thousand blast furnaces, Ogunn's fist smashed the top of Sven's head. The gray gryphon crumpled and lay still.

Seeing her gryphon fall sent Sigrid into a rage. She charged at Ogunn, axes swinging. Knocking aside her blows with one arm, the black golem reached down and plucked her off the ground by the neck. For a moment, Sigrid's eyes — wide as the iron fist choked the life out of her — met Eva's. She managed a tiny nod against Ogunn's grip.

Eva screamed and tried to jump from Fury as the gryphon pulled farther away from the island. Chel wrapped her arms around Eva and held her in the saddle.

Ogunn lifted Sigrid high above his head. She kicked one last time before her body went limp. The black golem tossed her to the ground.

Sigrid hit the earth in a crumpled heap beside Sven. Neither stirred.

Staring up at Eva with his raging crimson eyes, Ogunn waved a hand in farewell as Fury flew away.

Chapter
22

They flew throughout the night and well into the next day. When the gryphons could go no further, they half-landed and half-collapsed in a giant field of wildflowers. Eva and Chel slid from Fury's back in silence. Through the haze of fatigue and heartbreak, Eva managed to unsaddle Fury, letting the gear slide from the gryphons back into a pile on the ground. She slumped to the ground beside the gear and pulled her legs in tight to her chest. A shiver coursed through her, although the sun shone bright.

Tahl sat down next to her and wrapped his arm around her. "Eva…"

She shook her head. Ivan, Chel, and Wynn sat down nearby. All at once, like a great dam breaking, Eva felt tears she didn't know she had left in her pour out. Sobs rose from the others.

"Get some rest," Soot said after they'd cried themselves in a depressing silence. "I'll take the first watch."

Eva nodded, weary beyond measure. Despite the hurt inside, sleep overtook her and she slumped into oblivion.

The sun dipped down over the tree line to the west by the time Eva awakened. The rest were already up, going about a random assortment of chores — repairing gear, sharpening weapons, tending to wounds.

Eva looked over at the three gryphons resting nearby, in mourning as much as the humans. Sven's absence brought another fresh wave of pain. Sigrid, who had fought together with Eva through everything, Sigrid who feared nothing and no one — was gone.

Eva rose and walked to Fury. The gryphon stood and uttered a soft peep as she drew close. She half fell into him, wrapping her arms around his feathered neck. When she pulled back, the pain and hurt were clear in his eyes as well. The two of them had known Sigrid and Sven almost as long as each other — flown together, fought together, suffered and triumphed together.

When Eva turned around the others were watching her, as if she had an answer, as if she could be the strong one. Fortunately, Soot took charge. He was Eva's last remaining pillar of strength.

"Ogunn needs the stones as much as he needed Seppo," the smith said. "The Smelterborn won't be able to make it back to Palantis before we can fly there — there's still a chance."

A chance. Sigrid hadn't had a chance against Ogunn. Had she known that? Had she known that saving Eva's life would cost her own? Eva knew if she'd just listened to Soot and Seppo, just done what the others told her and left, that Sigrid would be alive. Every time she closed her eyes, Eva saw Sigrid hanging from Ogunn's grasp before being cast to the ground like a straw doll, her life snuffed out in a few heartbeats.

"Eva!" Soot said, in a loud, but not unkind voice that momentarily drew Eva from her thoughts. She shook her head and looked up, trying to focus on the setting sun shining off her foster father's bald head. "I know it hurts. But we can make their sacrifice mean something if we destroy the First Forge."

Eva nodded. Inside, however, she wondered how high the cost of victory would be. Sigrid and Sven, Aleron and Sunflash, Adelar and Justicar, the soldiers and gryphons at the Talon, the Scrawls in the meadow and countless others — the blood price was already terrible to reckon.

Eva did her best to edge those thoughts aside as Soot continued.

"We're only a few days from the coast, I think," Soot said. "And we're not that far south of Palantis. If we keep an eye out for other Smelterborn patrols and Runefolk, we should be able to make it to the ocean without a fight. They'll know we're coming, though. Be expecting us now."

Eva tried to sort through everything Soot had just said and she saw the same empty looks on the others' faces as well.

"Now is not the time to grieve," Soot said. "Right now, we've got to get back on the gryphons and —"

"For sky's sake, do you hear yourself?" Tahl yelled. "Have you no heart? We just lost one of our riders, one of our sisters, and you're talking about getting to that storm-cursed island like nothing happened!"

Soot gritted his teeth and grabbed Tahl by the collar. Veins popped out the sides of his bald head as he lifted the slighter, younger man off the ground.

"I've lost plenty of friends myself, *boy*. We left Seppo back there too, if you don't remember. Either we sit here and wallow in our misery or we can make their lives count for something."

He finished speaking and released Tahl, with a shove. The younger man stepped forward and raised his fists, but Eva jumped between them, hands pushing both of their chests.

"Stop!" she screamed. "*Stop it!* This doesn't solve anything. We have enough enemies to fight without fighting each other."

Eva looked at Tahl and Soot then the others. "We've got to keep moving. We're going to finish this. For Sigrid… for everyone who has died because of Ogunn and his Smelterborn."

The days blended together in a wash of grief. When at last they reached the coast, Eva stared out over the empty horizon but felt no joy. Burdened with guilt, she wanted nothing more than to destroy the First Forge — any thought of what might come after that evaded her. Home? Sigrid and Sven would never go home.

Soot joined her on the beach while the others set up camp. Together, they listened to the sound of the slate-colored waves crashing into the shore.

"Never thought I'd see this damn ocean again," he said. A long pause ensued.

"It's hard," he continued, "to live with all those thoughts and feelings after the people attached to them are gone. I used to curse the day we came to this storming place, but then you know what I realized?"

Eva shook her head, throat tight, unable to speak even if she had known what to say.

"I realized," Soot said in a thick voice. "That if I'd never come here, I'd never have been able to raise you. And that…that alone makes it all worth it, Eva."

Unable to stem the tide, Eva burst into tears. She wrapped herself around Soot and buried her face in his broad chest. Eventually, his reassuring pats calmed her.

"I know things look awful grim right now, but we'll get through it," Soot assured her. "You know what they say about the strongest steel?"

Eva lifted her face to look at her foster father. It was a line he'd repeated hundreds of times to her growing up. She knew it by heart:

"It comes from the heaviest hammer blows and hottest fires."

They took turns scouting in pairs up the coast, flying only a couple hours away at a time to ensure the path ahead was clear. The weather grew warmer and a haze settled over the area, obscuring everything beyond a half-mile or so. Eva worried they would get lost in the hot, sweltering smog that smelled of hot iron and ash, or come across a band of Smelterborn with no warning.

Their scant luck held out until, one day, the winds picked up and blew the haze out to sea. And there is was: hardly more than a smudge to the north, a collection of white ridges sticking out above the ocean.

"There you have it," Soot said. "We're still a couple days away from the closest point to the shore, but that's Palantis."

They soon spotted a number of Smelterborn patrols and were forced into a hiding place in the ruins of some building that Eva guessed had once been a dock warehouse of some kind. Although the roof had fallen in, the walls looked to be strong and it was large enough to fit them and the gryphons with room to spare. Most of the other ruins around them were little more than rubble and random blocks of stone, giving them a good view of their surroundings so that the Smelterborn couldn't catch them unawares.

At first and last light, two riders flew out, soaring high above and searching for any sign of Ogunn and his Smelterborn returning with Seppo. Eva volunteered for the duty as often as she could. Alone with Fury, high in the sky, her problems, grief, and worries seemed distant. Each time they landed, however, it all came rushing back.

Smoke rose from Palantis day and night, spreading its murk out across the ocean and often obscuring the island until a sea breeze blew it away. It seemed to Eva that the land itself was trying in vain to erase all memory of the Palantines.

When Ogunn and Seppo failed to appear in the next few days they agreed to make for the island and wait there.

"The island is about ten miles long and three wide," Soot said. "The main citadel, or what we guessed was the palace, is on the highest hill to the east. The city is ringed by a series of walls separating each district as you move uphill toward the palace. There are four in all. The first is a seawall — not much left of it. The next separates what was probably farmland from the third level, which had the largest number of ruins. We found Seppo inside a cavern within the third wall. The First Forge, if I had to guess, is somewhere within the third ring of the city as well."

"Where is the best place to land?" Tahl asked.

Soot tapped on the right side of his rough map representing the eastern beach, behind the palace. "Here, definitely," he said. "There's a narrow gap at low tide between the farmlands and the cliffs still above water. I'm guessing it will be the least guarded spot on the island, at least until Ogunn returns."

Eva studied the map, running over the plan in her mind. The full moon was only a couple days away, meaning they'd have enough light to fly after dark, depending on the winds and smog.

"We'll go tonight and check it out," she said. Wynn opened her mouth, no doubt to ask who 'we' would be, but Eva cut her off. "All of us, together."

"Sounds like a plan to me," Soot said. "Better rest up. Once we're on the island, we're in for it whether we like it or not."

Chapter 23

Several restless hours passed by until the sun finally fell over the hills and trees to the west. The lack of any distinguishable landmarks left Eva anxious, almost as much as she had been crossing the Endless. She longed for the sight of the Gyr and the Windswepts towering into the sky, their steep slopes a familiar guide.

When night fell completely, they ventured out. Finding the coast clear, they mounted the gryphons and Eva felt a sharp pang from the all-too-familiar absence of Sven and Sigrid. Pushing these feelings aside in an attempt to focus on the task at hand, Eva clicked her tongue and Fury leaped into the air, scattering beach pebbles and sand in his wake.

The night remained mild, but as they climbed higher and higher to stay out of sight, Eva felt a chill in the air. She took a deep breath, glad to be free of the smoke and haze where everything felt cleaner and fresher.

They reached Palantis faster than Eva expected. It was the first time for everyone but Soot to see it up close. Even amidst the decay and destruction, the ruined glory that had once been the capital city of all Altaris could still be imagined. Now, however, the home of the wisest, wealthiest and most powerful people of an empire was but a sad skeleton of its former majesty and glory. Only one tower still stood at full height — a stubborn, ancient, and weathered lord scowling down on the pathetic remnants of his subjects.

A waterfall sprang from the rock just below the palace gates and ran in a straight line down through each of the city's rings until it emptied into the ocean. Just as Soot said, Eva saw the skeletons of the walls, crumbling into mounds. Even so, they formed almost perfect circles an equal distance apart all the way around the island. Eva couldn't help but admire the craftsmanship that had gone into building the city.

But no matter how skilled its master builders might have been, Palantis still bowed before all-powerful time. The city's once-magnificent structures were reduced to piles of stone, cracked and overgrown with vines and moss. The outer, undeveloped land sported overgrown, tangled orchards and weed-choked fields. Eva noticed the trees were barren, black and gray as if they'd been burnt and never recovered. Even the fields, separated into square parcels by low, stone walls, only grew clumps of faded, gray-brown grass. Palantis, it seemed, had poisoned itself.

As expected, Smelterborn filled the ruins. Many stood almost motionless and Eva mistook the first few for statues. Others were hard at work, clearing aside the rubble to fill in the many gaps and fallen parts of the inner wall. For all their might as war machines, the Smelterborn's building prowess left much to be desired. In many places, Eva saw the golems' primitive patch jobs had already collapsed. It seemed fitting that such instruments of death and destruction would be incapable of creating.

The First Forge sat in the middle of the ruined palace courtyard, a monstrous furnace crafted from the same hue as the Smelterborns' armor. Harsh runes circled the domed top and ran down the side, glowing orange and red. Eva shuddered, thinking of the death and destruction the structure had caused in its lifetime. The smelter burned so hot she could feel the heatwaves in the air, like an updraft in the middle of summer. Eva's Wonder pulsed and vibrated, offering no comfort for the darkness seeping over her spirit. She looked away but knew the sight would be burned in her mind forever.

Just as Soot predicted, the small beach below the eastern cliffs was empty. After two passes to be sure, Eva directed Fury into his descent.

On the ground, Eva patted her faithful gryphon, taking note of the sweat marks darkening Fury's fur from the arduous flight. Fury opened his beak and panted. Carroc and Lucia were in a similar state. Eva's heart went out to the proud creatures as she noticed again the toll the journey had taken on them.

"Have a rest, boy," she said, scratching Fury behind the ears. "You've earned it."

Crossing the pale, slate-colored sand, the thought crossed Eva's mind that, one way or the other, this was it. All the heartbreaking miles and battles came down to one thing: destroying the First Forge or dying in the attempt. One look at Soot, Ivan, Chel, Wynn, and Tahl told her they all harbored similar thoughts.

They made camp at the base of the cliffs, picking their way through giant slabs of fallen rock until they found a bit of high ground large enough for the gryphons to lie down. Unable to light a fire for fear of being seen, they shared a dinner of cold, stale rations. Eva realized they would be hard-pressed to avoid starvation if they had to make a return journey. She told herself to worry about one thing at a time.

"What do we do now?" Chel asked.

Soot and Eva shared a look. "You're the one who's been here before," Eva said. "How do we find the First Forge?"

"And how do we destroy it?" Wynn asked.

Soot jerked a thumb at Ivan. "That's a question for the Scrawl."

They all turned expectantly to Ivan.

"How in the tempest would I know?" he said, throwing his tattooed hands in the air. When they continued to stare, he rolled his eyes and paused, gathering his thoughts. "Well…this is only a guess, mind you — but I would guess Ogunn will wait for the full moon before he tries to work the magic. The runes and kennings are more potent at certain times of year: full moons, new moons, solstices, changing season — you get the idea. Plus he still needs the two stones."

"The full moon is tomorrow night," Chel said, pointing to the waxing moon overhead.

"And I'll wager it won't take long for the Smelterborn to figure out the stones are on the island," Soot added. "Ogunn will turn every golem out to find us."

"So we've got one night to figure out how to save all of Altaris," Wynn said.

"If that," Tahl said.

Ivan gave a dry laugh and shook his head. "Well, if that's all, it shouldn't be too hard."

Chel, seemingly sensing Eva's distress, leaned forward and clasped Eva's arm. Her calm, reassuring grip gave Eva strength. "We will do this, Eva-lyn."

"Together," Tahl said.

Wynn nodded. "For Sigrid."

"For Seppo," Soot said.

In spite of all they'd been through, Eva managed a smile. "Let's get to work, then."

Over the course of the next hour, they concocted a plan. Given that Eva and Ivan possessed the only means of destroying the Smelterborn between Ivan's magic and Eva's Wonder and sword, the plan hinged on them distracting the golems while the others freed Seppo. Once the fight began, the gryphons would drop in overhead. Between daylight and the full moon, they had no chance of using Fury and the rest in any sort of sneak attack — the Smelterborn would see them long before they could strike unless the golems were already distracted.

"It would sure help if that sky-cursed bucket head had told us how to destroy the First Forge before he went and got himself captured."

Although he acted gruff and perturbed at the golem, Eva knew Soot worried about Seppo. No one had said it aloud, but they all had to have wondered: what would happen to Seppo when the First Forge was destroyed?

The pale moonlight provided plenty of light to scout the surrounding beach while the gryphons rested. Dividing into groups of two, they spread out and were careful to remain at the base of the cliff, away from any searching eyes overhead.

"Hey!" Wynn said in a loud whisper, rushing to gather the others a few minutes into their search. "You've…gotta….see this!"

They followed her and Ivan to a small cave opening, tall enough for the humans to enter — Soot would have to bend over a bit — but definitely too small for the gryphons unless they crawled in. Eva peered inside but couldn't make out anything past the line of moonlight at the cavern's edge.

"Where do you think it goes?" Ivan wondered aloud.

"You know anything about this?" Eva asked Soot.

"Hmm," Eva's foster father rubbed the scruff on his face. "There were a series of caverns beneath the palace. That's where Celina found her gauntlet and Aleron that sword you've got. Might be this connects in with them. There were too many to explore, so it's hard to say."

"Doesn't that mean it will be watched?" Tahl asked. "If Ogunn can sense the stones won't he try to set up an ambush?"

"Still worth checking out," Soot said. "If we can find a backdoor in — well, that's better than rushing in, swords swinging at an army of Smelterborn. Besides, if I remember right, most of the tunnels were too small for golems."

After ensuring the gryphons would stay once their riders disappeared into the cavern — it took some persuading to get Fury to calm down and accept being left behind — Eva took the lead. She held her Wonder cupped in her hands to illuminate the tunnel, shielding the light so they could barely see where they were going. Ivan followed close behind, a tiny ball of flame cupped in his hands. Soot brought up the rear after the others.

The tunnel ran up at a moderate incline for a good distance, the walls square and perfectly cut, just like the halls and passages in the Gyr. Unlike the Gyr, however, there were no crystal lanterns — either lighted or broken — along the way. Even with the dimmed light of Eva's Wonder and Ivan's flame, they tripped and stumbled, stifling curses. Even the slightest sound carried down the tunnels.

Eventually, the path leveled out and split into a chamber with four different exits, in addition to the one they'd entered from. Rune carvings marked the wall by each. Whereas the tunnel they'd just left had been cut with precision, the runes were jagged and chipped, as if someone had gouged them out of the rock with their bare hands, like digging into half-dried clay.

"Which way?" Eva whispered to Ivan.

The Scrawl walked up to each symbol and studied them in the flickering light of his rune fire. Eva saw his face darken upon the further examination.

"These are foul characters," he muttered. "Old blood magic, like we found in the depths of the Gyr."

"I'd say we're on the right track then," Soot said. "But which one do we take?"

Ivan studied the runes for another moment before selecting the tunnel second to the right. "This is our safest bet. I don't understand the two on the left, and I definitely don't want to find out what's down the far right path."

Recalling the series of traps in the bowels of the Gyr, Eva let Ivan lead the way to scan the walls for further markings and signs of snares and pitfalls they might set off. During the short journey she'd undertaken in the bottom of the Gyr with Tahl and Sigrid during her first year training to be a rider, they'd encountered collapsing floors, fake bridges, panels of spikes and a whole variety of ways to die in the mountain's depths. One look at Tahl told Eva he was thinking the same thing.

The walls on the path Ivan chose were rough and gouged from the stone in complete contrast to the craftsmanship on display in the previous tunnel. The air, growing hotter and thicker, was filled with the same foul smoke they'd watched billow off the island over the past few days. Soon they all dripped with sweat and Eva would have given anything for a breath of fresh air.

All of a sudden, Ivan held up his non-flaming hand, and Eva almost ran into it. Wynn cursed under her breath as she ran into Eva's back. Ivan lifted a finger to his lips and then held his other fire-filled hand up to his face and whispered something to the flame. It shrank further, giving off only the faintest flicker of light. Eva took the hint and tucked her Wonder into her shirt, feeling the darkness press in around them as she did so.

"There's something ahead," Ivan said in a low voice. "Something moving."

Holding her breath, Eva strained to pick up any sounds of something approaching ahead of them. A Smelterborn, she knew, could never fit in these tunnels, nor move silently but who knew what else might be waiting down here in the dark?

A strange, muffled whirring and clicking sound drifted toward them then went silent just as fast. They fell into complete silence listening for further noises. Eva felt her heart pounding in her ears, sensed her shallow breath hissing out of her, felt the beads of sweat trickling down her face. Silence reigned.

Just as she was about to nudge Ivan onward, the sound started again, lasting this time for a few seconds more. Ivan looked at her and nodded down at the flame in his hand as if to ask if Eva wanted him to increase the light.

Eva shook her head, although she wanted nothing more than to see farther than an arm's length in front of them. The clicking sounded again — a tapping noise against the rock. There was no doubting whatever it might be was getting louder and closer.

Eva drew her sword, aware of its limited use in the tight space. As she did, Ivan hissed. Down the tunnel, dozens of tiny, yellow eyes stared back at them from the darkness.

Chapter
24

The eyes disappeared.

"Light now?" Ivan asked, a trace of panic in his voice. He stepped back and balled his other hand into a fist.

"Not yet," Eva said, heart pounding even faster. Her arms felt like willow branches and she squeezed her sword hilt tighter.

The rustling grew louder, like dozens of tiny hammers clinking against the tunnel floor. The volume increased as well. Eva peered into the darkness, but the yellow lights were gone.

"Now?" Ivan asked, apprehension thick in his voice.

Eva hesitated. Behind her, the others shifted, trying to get into some semblance of a fighting formation in the close quarters. All of a sudden, the sound came not only from in front of them but behind as well.

"*Now?*" Ivan asked, voice cracking.

Eva tossed the decision back and forth faster than the tapping and clinking noise echoing all around them. And then dozens of yellow eyes appeared.

"Now!"

A blinding flash filled the tunnel as Ivan summoned the fire kenning and a ball of flame burst into his hand. The orange light revealed a horde of dog-sized mechanical spiders scuttling on the floors, walls, and ceiling toward them.

Eva bit back a scream as Ivan blasted the closest off the top of the tunnel with a fireball and summoned another to shoot at one on the floor. Eva heard the others struggling in the tunnel behind her, knocking into each other and the tunnel walls in the process of trying to fight off the spiders.

"Let me through!" Eva said, trying to push her way past Chel, Wynn, Tahl and, hardest of all, Soot. The burly smith swung his hammer, smashing a spider into a thousand bits of metal, gears, and cogs. Sliding past him, Eva stabbed out with her sword. One cut from the rune blade was all it took — the sword split the spider in half with ease. But they were fast. Eva barely managed to hold them off as dozens of the mechanical arachnids swarmed forward, reaching with long legs and razor-sharp pincers capable of shredding them to pieces.

Each moment stretched by as Eva cut through the spiders until she pinned the last of the swarm to the ground. It gave a feeble clicking noise through its metal mandible and shuddered before its many limbs went still. Eva sucked in a deep breath, sheathing her sword and shook her aching arms.

"Lovely," Ivan said, kicking the blackened shell of one of the mechanical spiders. "We've got giant golems ready to pulverize us above ground and if that doesn't work, there's these little horrors crawling around to flay off our skin in the dark."

"This don't bode well," Soot said. "There weren't anything like these last time."

"It would seem the Smelterborn have not been idle, then," Chel said, doing her best to step around the metal corpses. She, Wynn, and Tahl hadn't been able to do much in the close quarters but keep an eye out for any of the spiders trying to surround Ivan and Eva.

"Let's keep moving," Eva said. "We've made too much noise."

Squeezing her way past the others to the front of the line with Ivan again, Eva followed the Scrawl. She saw the strain on Ivan's face in the flicker of his rune-flame, the cost of the short but strenuous fight.

The tunnel twisted and turned past dozens of offshoots and dead ends, forcing them to backtrack multiple times until Eva hardly knew where they were or how to get back to the beach. As they continued deeper into the rock, the stone and air around them grew hotter and hotter. Eva started to wonder if they'd brought enough water or if they would lose their way and perish of thirst.

At last, Ivan's light blended with an orange glow ahead which grew brighter and brighter until the Scrawl could douse his flame. Creeping forward, they saw the tunnel widen ahead. Eva held up a hand to keep the others back while she and Ivan peered around, searching for the source of the light.

The tunnel opened up into a large cavern, a sort of junction for dozens of other passages. From their vantage point high above the cavern floor, Eva saw dozens of Smelterborn working, hammering and heating rods of metal. They formed neat, orderly lines, each golem assigned to a different task. It took Eva a moment to realize they were working in a long line, each Smelterborn crafting a different part of the weapon, all the way down to a section of Shadowstalkers who handled the finishing work and sharpened the blades. The final resulting weapons were crude but made with incredible efficiency.

Eva raised a hand to wipe the sweat from her face — the heat from the room was stifling, making it hard to breathe beneath her chain mail, which felt like a hot blanket. Sliding back on their stomachs, Ivan and Eva rejoined the rest to report what they'd seen.

"I know where we are!" Soot said. "That room is part of the caverns we explored when we came to Palantis the first time." He nodded to the sword at Eva's side. "Your father found that in one of the antechambers. There were others, but none of us bothered bringing any — they all looked like a bunch of useless relics."

"Bet you wish you'd grabbed them now," Ivan muttered.

"We'll have to backtrack," Eva said before Soot could retort. "There's no way we can get across to another tunnel without being spotted and —"

"Wait up there!" Wynn hissed. Eva shot her an annoyed glance but waited for the girl to speak. "You're telling me there might be more enchanted weapons that kill the Smelterborn lying around and we're just going to wander off to look for another passage?"

"We don't have much time," Soot said. "But the girl's got a point — there's a good chance some of the other relics could do the same damage."

"If Ogunn has not destroyed them," Chel pointed out.

Thinking back on their journey through the tunnels, Eva tried to figure out how long it had been since they'd left the gryphons on the beach. At least three or four hours, and there was a good chance it would take them even longer than that to find their way out. They were running out of time.

"If we can dig up even one more weapon, it would be worth it," Tahl said.

Eva gave a reluctant nod. "Where do we go from here?" she asked Soot.

The smith thought for a long moment and then gave a couple of different guesses where he thought there might be other rune weapons. "Stick to the tunnels small enough the Smelterborn can't get in," he said. "If I remember right, that's where most of the human-sized stuff was anyway, this must've been an armory even before the Smelterborn took it over."

Although Eva hated to do it, she realized they would have to split up to cover the most ground in their limited time. Since Ivan and Eva were the only two with surefire means to kill Smelterborn, they headed the two groups. Soot went with the Scrawl and took Wynn, which left Chel and Tahl with Eva.

After backtracking to a previous split in the tunnels, Ivan marked runes into the walls for direction and they agreed to meet back in two hours' time, regardless of whether they found anything in their explorations or not. To mark the time, Wynn and Tahl did the only thing they could to keep track in the sunless tunnels: counting.

Before parting, they all agreed that if the other party wasn't back they would only wait a short time before making their way out to the beach.

"It's the only way," Soot said when Eva began to argue. "If we can find something to help us we've got to take the chance. But we can't sit around and wait for one another — the risk is too great."

After a quick goodbye and round of luck-wishing, they separated. Eva, Tahl, and Chel chose a path to the right of the one that led into the forge area. The others took a path to the left. Soon, the faint scraping of boots faded and they were alone, guided only by the soft glow of Eva's Wonder cupped in her hands.

The tunnels here were once again smooth and straight, cut at angles rather than winding and curving. Eva thought back to the spider golems and wondered if they'd carved the other tunnel, digging away with their pincers and mandibles, creating an entirely new network of caves. She suppressed the thought of hundreds of machinations scampering around in the dark and focused on Soot's directions.

After an hour or so passed, according to Tahl's count, they came across several rooms that looked to have once been a barracks or soldier's quarters, not dissimilar to those inside the Gyr. There were even crystal lamps fashioned to the wall, although none of them gave off any light.

A search through the first room found nothing but dust. Everything seemed to be rotted away. In the neighboring room, however, Eva spotted the corroded, pitted remnants of a suit of armor. She reached for the tarnished breastplate, frowning at the strange design and jumped back. The cracked and yellowed remnants of a skeleton poked out beneath the armor.

When she'd recovered from the unexpected scare, a look around revealed other soldiers' remains. They looked hundreds of years old, only fragments of bones, skulls, and armor preserved by the cave remaining.

"If this was the garrison, there should be weapons around," Eva said to the others.

They spread out and combed the tight quarters to no avail. Eva found a dagger hilt and what looked like the rusted remains of a sword blade, but they were so rusted away they wouldn't have done any good against a mortal opponent, let alone the Smelterborn.

"I wonder when the last time was that a living human walked in here," Tahl said.

The thought made Eva pause. She felt a small pang of guilt for rooting through the resting place of these people, no matter how long they'd been dead. They searched a few more minutes without any results. That, combined with Eva's newfound desire to leave the remains in peace, sent them on their way.

Unlike the Gyr, whose tunnels often opened up into wide corridors and various rooms, the passageways beneath the palace were barely wide enough for two people to pass through. The thought crossed Eva that the ancient Palantines must not have been very tall because her head almost scraped the tops of the walls. Tahl had to duck and she couldn't imagine what a pain it must be for Soot to wander through such confined spaces.

Although the heat from the forge faded, it never went away. Thankfully, they saw no more sign of the golem spiders and Eva wondered if they kept themselves to the darker, cooler parts of the caverns, even though they'd clearly been crafted by someone or something.

Their continued search yielded nothing. After crossing into a side corridor and coming upon their own tracks on the ground, the three decided to head back to the meeting area while they had the chance to retrace their steps. After all their searching, they had only sweat, thirst and a layer of dust and grit to show for it.

"It does not matter, Eva-lyn," Chel said, sensing Eva's disappointment. "We do not need more magic weapons to kill the iron men. It will be okay."

Eva had her doubts, but she bit back a discouraging comment and hurried their pace. An anxious feeling overtook her and she longed to be reunited with the rest of the group and assured they were all safe and sound. It didn't take long, now that they were no longer searching every room and side chamber to get back to the arranged meeting place.

No one was there.

Eva's heart sank and she berated herself for letting the group split up. "I knew we should have stayed together," she said out loud, slapping a hand against the rock wall. "I knew it. I just —"

Tahl took her shoulders in both hands. "Deep breath," he said. "We don't know anything has happened yet. Maybe they found something or —"

"Or maybe they were captured or killed," Eva said, in a flat voice.

Tahl gave her a gentle squeeze. "We don't know that. Let's just wait a few minutes and see."

Eva heaved a deep breath and nodded reluctantly. But the waiting proved excruciating.

With nothing to do to preoccupy their time, the three sat on the stone ground and checked their weapons. The task only took a few minutes and left them with nothing else to do but worry. Eva's mind conjured dozens of different things that could have happened. What if one of them were hurt? What if they'd gotten lost? What if? What if?

"I can't take it anymore," she said after what was probably a much shorter amount of time than it felt like. "There's no point in us waiting here, we might as well follow their tracks in and meet up with them. That way we'll know for sure."

Both Chel and Tahl looked like they wanted to argue, but seeing the determined look on Eva's face they just nodded and followed her down the tunnel.

Like the passages they'd gone down, the amount of ash and dust on the ground made it easy to follow the path the others took. When they came to the first intersection, Tahl saw another of Ivan's runes glowing light blue on the wall and felt grateful for the Scrawl's foresight. However, the sight of the marking made Eva realize that if the others were smart enough to mark their path, the chances they'd gotten lost were slim. Once more, Eva thought back to all the traps they'd encountered searching the bottom caverns of the Gyr and feared the worst.

Unlike the passages Eva, Tahl, and Chel searched, the corridor the others went down didn't seem to branch off into any rooms or antechambers. They continued to follow the tracks, pointed in the right direction whenever they came to a junction thanks to Ivan's runes on the wall. Eva wondered how long before the markings would fade and hurried her pace even more.

Much to their chagrin, the air grew hotter again and Eva realized they were swinging back around toward the Smelterborn armory. Eva found small comfort that the tunnels remained too small for the Smelterborn to fit through. There was no sign of the mechanical spiders anywhere, either, or any other struggle.

After an hour, Eva's stomach twisted as if full of snakes. She didn't dare call out and they'd seen and heard nothing to suggest they were getting any closer to Ivan, Soot, and Wynn. She knew both of the others were wondering if they should go back to the meeting place and part of her wondered if the group might have circled around another route back and were even now back at the juncture, waiting for them to return.

"Eva…" Tahl began after they continued into what felt like their second hour.

"I know," she snapped. "Just a bit farther and then I promise, we'll turn back."

Inside, Eva doubted they would come across anything but wasn't willing to turn back yet. The tunnel widened. Eva's stomach clenched even tighter when she realized the corridor they were in now could definitely fit a Smelterborn. To make matters worse, the ash and dust had been blown away by a slight breeze ahead, erasing all traces of their friends' footsteps.

"Eva," Tahl said again, this time in a much firmer voice.

"We should go back, Eva-lyn," Chel added, although her tone was more nervous than insistent.

"I know," Eva said, still walking forward. " I just —"

She paused, mouth dry as the dim light from her Wonder illuminated an object on the floor. Rushing forward she knelt down, confirming her worst fears — Soot's hammer.

The others joined her. No one spoke as they stared down at the smith's weapon.

"Maybe…he left it here to mark the way so they didn't risk a rune on the wall?" Tahl said. Eva could tell by his tone that he didn't believe it. They were in a long, straight hallway, with no offshoot or any possible way to get lost.

"It could be morning," Chel said, rubbing her sleep-deprived, reddened eyes. "We may have less than a day to go back."

"I don't care!" Eva hissed with a venom that surprised her. Chel took a step back, the hurt look on her face falling into a scowl.

Eva paused and took a deep breath. "I'm sorry. But if there's still time, we've got to keep going."

Continuing down the hall, it wasn't long before they came across another sign of struggle: a Windsworn sword snapped off just above the hilt. Tahl picked it up, face pale even in the darkness.

"Wynn's."

Eva drew her sword but the faintly glowing runes offered no comfort in the heart of their enemy's domain.

They continued down the hall, which by now had grown into a corridor three times their height and almost twice that wide. The size was similar to some of the main halls in the Gyr, complete with columns down either side. Although the large passage looked abandoned, Eva kept the light from her Wonder cupped as best she could, afraid of revealing their location to searching golems.

The light spilled on a large form in the middle of the hall. Eva froze, heart pounding. After a moment's studying, they walked forward to find the shell of a Smelterborn, followed by two more beyond. Their helmeted faces were still wrapped in ice.

"Ivan," Eva muttered.

Bright orange light waved and flickered ahead out of a side passage, with an entrance wide enough for a gryphon to pass through wings extended. It was taller than three Smelterborn standing atop one another. Eva moved to one side of the hall, behind the columns, Tahl and Chel close behind. They flitted from one column to the next, hiding in the shadows.

At last, they reached the corner. Eva felt overwhelmed by the heat — even the stone wall was too hot to leave her hand on for more than a few moments. Blinking the sweat from her eyes, Eva peered around the gigantic arch.

The chamber looked like a larger version of the armory complete with anvils and a furnace several times bigger than the one in Soot's smithy back in Gryfonesse. Smelterborn crowded the room, facing the opposite direction. They were circled around something, but Eva couldn't see what.

"Are they in there?" Tahl asked from behind her.

Eva shook her head, hair lank and soaked with sweat like she'd been out in the rain. "I can't tell, they've —."

"Welcome," a familiar, booming voice said, its words echoing throughout the chamber. "Welcome to the heart of my empire. I thank you for delivering the Deimos to me — perhaps I will make your deaths quick in return for this service."

The Smelterborn jerked to attention and Eva got a clear shot through their ranks. Wrapped in chains, Soot, Wynn, and Ivan knelt before Ogunn. The dark golem paced back and forth before them.

Eva felt a burning against her chest and yanked her Wonder away from her skin. As soon as she touched the stone, Ogunn's helmeted head shot toward them. Although Eva ducked away, she could feel his fiery eyes on her.

"There you are, skulking about my palace like a little rat," he said in a rumbling voice. "Seize them!"

Chapter 25

*R*un!" Eva shouted, turning and sprinting away.

Tahl and Chel followed close behind and together their feet pounded down the long dark hallway. Out of the corner of her eye, Eva saw dark shapes descending from the pillars on either side of the hall. Looking up revealed Shadowstalkers leaping from the heights where they'd been hiding.

Eva realized they'd fell right into the trap and cursed herself for being a fool twice over. Ahead, a line of scout golems ran toward them, metal hands empty of weapons, their arms stretched out to catch their prey.

Drawing her sword in mid-stride, Eva cut through the lead golem. Tahl and Chel managed to stay with her, dodging past the grasping arms of the other Smelterborn. Farther down the hall, Eva spotted more moving to intercept them. They were being surrounded.

The next golems forced Eva to a halt but she still manged to cut through two of the Shadowstalkers. A sharp cry rang out and Eva spun to find Chel on the ground, stabbing hopelessly at a Smelterborn that had its hand wrapped around her ankle, pulling her backward.

"Keep going!"

Eva ignored Tahl's shout and slashed through the golem's arm before stabbing it in its helmeted face. The Smelterborn fell down, its shadow shooting away as Tahl pulled Chel to her feet.

But the act had cost them precious time they didn't have to spare. The other Smelterborn circled around, hemming them in. Eva lashed out at them, Tahl and Chel pressed close to her, back to back. Seeing the effect of her weapon, the golems hesitated. A series of thunderclaps burst through the passage and Eva saw Ogunn running toward them, as fast as the Shadowstalkers.

Desperate, Eva searched for a way out. In the darkness she could see nothing beyond the burning eyes of the Smelterborn.

With nothing else to turn to, Eva pulled her Wonder free. The stone gave a weak flicker.

"Come one," Eva growled, squeezing it in a death grip. "Come on, shine!"

As if on cue, bright gold and rose-colored lights burst forth between Eva's clenched fingers. The golems staggered backward, shielding their eyes. It was all they needed.

Eva cut her way past two golems, creating a gap in the circle of Smelterborn for them to leap through. Ogunn's voice grew louder and closer behind them.

"Catch them! CATCH THEM!"

The thunderous noise sent bits of rock from the ceiling. Eva's ears rang and she willed her burning legs to move faster, begged her aching lungs to suck in just one more breath. The light of the Wonder stone revealed the smaller passage less than a hundred paces away.

Risking a glance over her shoulder, Eva saw Ogunn gaining on them. Recovered from the stone's effects, the Shadowstalkers resumed their chase as well. Eva allowed herself to believe they had a chance.

For some reason, Eva noticed the many cracks and uneven spots in the floor, minor details that hadn't been a problem when they were creeping in the shadows, but now posed a serious threat as they sprinted over the broken ground.

Just as she leaped over yet another treacherous crack, Tahl yelled and went down hard to Eva's left.

Eva skidded to a halt, boots sliding on the loose rock and dirt. Tahl pulled himself to his feet, holding one foot off the ground.

"Come on, I've got you!" Eva managed, gasping for air. She pulled on Tahl's arm but he pushed her away.

"Won't…make it," he said through gritted teeth.

"I'm not leaving you!" Eva screamed.

Chel stepped between then shoved Eva away.

"Go, Eva-lyn!" her adopted sister yelled. "You are our last hope. You must run!"

Eva remained frozen in place, eyes darting from Tahl's pain stricken face to the approaching Smelterborn. She leaned forward and gave him a quick kiss, then nodded at Chel.

"I'll come back for you, I promise!"

Eva ran.

New strength surge through her and Eva hurtled across the broken ground like she'd never ran before. She didn't look back. She didn't heed the booming iron footsteps, drawing closer. She focused all her attention on the smaller side passage ahead.

Twenty paces away now.

The ground rumbled beneath Eva's feet as a Smelterborn — most likely Ogunn — closed in.

Ten paces.

A gust of wind behind her back told Eva one of the golems had just missed her.

Her lungs burned like a blast furnace, her legs screamed for respite.

Six paces.

Summoning the last vestiges of her strength Eva threw her sword ahead of her and dove into the smaller tunnel. She hit the ground hard but scrambled and managed to grab her weapon as a Smelterborn's metal hand wrapped around her ankle. As the golem dragged her backward, Eva twisted and lashed out blind with her sword, hoping she didn't cut her own foot off.

The blade struck metal and she felt the grip release. Swinging one more time to break free, Eva scampered on all fours down the tunnel, out of reach for the golems.

BOOM!

The ground quivered again. Dust and chips of stone fell from the ceiling as Ogunn struck the passage entrance. The dark golem forced his head and torso into the passage, one arm flailing around just out of reach.

"Pathetic human, do you think you can hide from me?" The golem roared. "Do you think —"

Overcome with rage, Eva screamed, a wild, gryphon-like sound and swung her sword as hard as she could at the golem's outstretched hand. The blade cut through Ogunn's fingers, severing the top half of his hand.

Ogunn's bellows of outrage were deafening. He jerked his hand back, the shorn-off fingers rusting away on the ground before Eva's eyes.

"*I WILL BURY YOU!*"

BOOM!

Eva felt the walls tremble as the gigantic golem rained down blow after blow on the tunnel entrance. Dust filled the air. Without waiting to see what happened, Eva turned and ran a dozen more paces down the hall. When she looked back, large slabs of stone fell free from the ceiling and walls. In moments, the passage was completely blocked. Only the occasional stone skittering across the ground broke the silence.

Sucking in a breath, Eva sobbed, her entire body quaking. The rune sword fell from her slackened hand and she slumped to the floor, gasping. Her Wonder fluttered like a candle in a windstorm, barely putting off enough light for her to see her feet.

Alone.

Completely alone, small, and scared.

Lord Vyr's words echoed in her mind: *What will do you, Evelyn? What you will do, when all hope seems lost and you find yourself alone in the darkness?*

Eva buried her face in her hands, overcome with hopelessness. A small sob escaped her and faded away into the surrounding abyss. She didn't feel like fighting anymore.

As if responding to her bleak thoughts, Eva's Wonder glowed, growing brighter and brighter until it lit up the tunnel like noonday for a dozen paces in each direction. Eva shaded her eyes and felt the calming warmth and light bask over her, filling her with strength and courage. She felt the encouragement of all those who'd helped bring her to right where she was now: her mother and father, her Uncle Adelar, and Sigrid as if they were standing beside her.

Eva grit her teeth and clenched her hands until her dirty, chipped nails cut into her palms. "I won't let you down," she said aloud.

It took several paces for Eva to realize she hadn't returned down the same passage they'd entered the hall from. In her haste to escape the Smelterborn, she'd dove into the closest narrow passage for protection. Now she was thinking with a clearer head, nothing looked familiar. Pushing aside another wave of despair, she held the Wonder stone out in front of her and did the only thing she could, aside from sitting down and waiting to die: she walked.

The tunnel twisted and wound in a mixture of smooth, square passages and rough tunnels carved from the rock. Whenever the pathway split, Eva wandered without reason. Even so, she thought clear enough to mark each junction and felt a tiny relief that she wasn't crossing her paths. She realized she was descending again, but had no idea in which direction — it would be impossible to tell if she was headed toward the eastern side of the island and the gryphons or another part of Palantis' underground caverns entirely.

Eva's mind wandered to Fury, Lucia and Carroc. She wished she had a way to let them know she was alive and trying to find them. They would wait for their riders indefinitely, but she could imagine what they must feel like, waiting on the outside of the tunnel with no idea what was happening or going on within.

As these fears took hold of her, Eva noticed the Wonder stone began to dim. Sensing the light fading with her resolve, Eva forced the fearful thoughts from her mind. The light grew and, for the first time, Eva noticed a line of runes along the wall at shoulder height.

How long had they been there?

Eva held her Wonder closer to the wall. She was certain there hadn't been runes like these throughout the entire labyrinth. Unlike the others marks here and there, closer inspection revealed lines of script running from ceiling to floor. The light from the Wonder seemed to reveal them, for when Eva pulled the light back they began to fade.

"Well, it's better than nothing," Eva said, the sound of her own voice in solitude strange to her ears.

Heartened by her discovery, Eva pushed on.

The rune walls continued for hundreds of paces and now the passage remained in almost a completely straight line. Although she still had no clue where she was, Eva felt hope coursing through her and picked up her pace to a jog. A faint blue glow appeared ahead, giving her pause. Eva continued at a steady, cautious pace. The blue light grew stronger and Eva rounded a sharp bend, finding herself in a small, round chamber with a domed ceiling.

A lantern hung suspended in the middle of the room. It was the source of the blue light but, unlike the magic lights in the Gyr, this was made of thousands of tiny cut and polished crystals. Eva saw rows and rows of runes carved all around the room, all the way up across the ceiling and circling the dome. In one corner sat a stone slab that looked like it might serve for a bed and against the opposite side she was a table and chair. She guessed the piles of dust sitting on shelves carved into the curved wall might have once been scrolls or books.

But it was the object in the middle of the room beneath the lantern that captured Eva's attention: a silver anvil, carved with the same blue, shining runes. A box of silver, inlaid with the most intricate work Eva had ever seen, sat atop it.

Eva tore her eyes away from the anvil and the box, looking up at the light. And then it hit her. The blue light, the vivid, cerulean glow, was the same hue as Seppo's eyes, the same color her Wonder often turned. Indeed, looking down at the stone in her hand, she saw it had changed to match the color of the lantern and runes within the room.

Trembling, Eva's fingers undid the clasp. The box's lid opened down the middle, like a pair of tiny doors. An empty slot sat under the lid, just the size of…

Eva felt a tingling sensation as she removed the Wonder stone from its golden chain. Holding it over the slot in the box, it looked like an exact fit. Eva's mouth went dry as she lowered the stone into the slot within the silver box. A perfect fit.

As soon as Eva's finger's left the stone, gold and rose-colored light burst forth. Throwing her hands over her eyes, Eva stumbled backwards and fell hard on the ground.

"Hello?"

Eva's eyes widened in shock and her hand went to her sword hilt. She wasn't alone.

Chapter 26

"H ello?"

The greeting sounded familiar but no one appeared.

Eva glanced around the room. She was alone.

Except for the box.

"Is someone there?" the voice asked

"What in the…" Eva trailed off. The box was *talking*. Talking in Seppo's voice!

"H-hello?" Eva replied in a shaky voice. "Seppo, is that you?"

The box ignored her question.

"Pronouncement 'Seppo' recognized. Rune sequence will begin."

Several of the runes on the outside of the box glowed before the voice continued.

"To whom it may concern: My name is Talus, Master Runesmith of the Palantine Empire. I am writing this message in the hopes that one day it will be found and my errors may be corrected. I began experimentation with rune engravings and enchanting upon inanimate objects almost two decades ago. My experimentations stemmed from a simple theory: if runes can augment living things such as people, animals, and plants, is there not a way to harness this same energy and power for inanimate objects?

"My tests began with weaponry. I sought to imbibe the written scripts for flame and ice into a sword blade. At first, these experiments all failed. After much toil, I realized that I could use certain combinations of scripts to augment power from the rune casters themselves.

"Upon this realization, I was successfully able to make armor and weapons inscribed with runes. Although they had no power of their own, they could store the energies of the rune casters. At the young age of fifty-three, barely an adult by Palantine standards, I became a famous and respected member of the Palantine Senate.

"Yet even after this success, I still retained the belief that there could be a way to transfer more than energy into objects. If a rune caster could put his summoned magic into an item, would it not be possible for him to transfer something else, such as a memory? I believed this could be used as a recording device, a way to store the collective knowledge of my people for generations to come. This box is proof that these experiments too, were a success. Alas, if I had only stopped there.

"It was at this time that I took upon a new apprentice, an extremely bright and talented young boy by the name of Ilmaren. I confess, his praise and flattering was something I reveled in. By this time, I had become one of the wealthiest members of the Palantine Senate, but this new apprentice of mine fueled the fire in me to do more.

"He posed a question to me, based on his readings of my earlier work: would it not be possible to craft objects that created their own power, rather than just storing it? Although not living things, wood, stone, and metals were still comprised of elemental matters.

"I told him this was the crux of my work, the one question I had not been able to answer. But I knew there must be some connection between the transference of rune magic and the transference of memory into objects. I had begun my life first as a smith and, as I experimented with rune carvings into inanimate objects in my early years, I returned to this vocation as part of my experimentation. Aside from my work with runes, I was also known as a master craftsman, aided, of course, by the rune tools I could create.

"After much pondering and experimenting, Ilmaren and I came to the conclusion that it might be possible not only to combine inanimate objects with rune power, but to also create a complete transference of conscious into these same objects. What we were working on, although we told no one of our secret experiments, was a way to create immortal life — a way to outlast the decay of the body and mind by placing one's collective within something that could never be destroyed by age or disease.

"I confess, our early experiments were immoral, to say the least. We used the bodies of the recently deceased and attempted to reanimate them with rune magic. However, a dead thing that was once living, we soon discovered, is not the same thing as something that has never lived. I thank all the gods that we failed at this juncture and altered our course.

"We returned to our research and, after months of calculations, I believed I had finally solved the problem. The transference had to occur with a live host, meaning the enchanting of an object combined with the transference of a live host would meld the two together.

"Naturally, the only thing that would work would be a suit of armor, as the person would have to be completely encased in the object. The person, wearing the enchanted and inscribed rune armor, would then be placed inside the smelter. The difference from our earlier tests was the inclusion of two runestones of opposing energies: the Aithos of Light and the Deimos of Darkness. These stones served to channel the rune magic and, we hoped, protect the person inside from the fires of the smelter. We named the completed structure the First Forge."

Here, there was a long pause and the voice of Talus/Seppo heaved a sigh.

"I, in my hubris, insisted that I test the process first, although Ilmaren volunteered numerous times. I told him I did not want to risk his life needlessly. In reality, I did not want him to succeed in my place and take even a fraction of the glory. And so I encased myself in a suit of armor, crafted specially for the experiment…."

Another long pause. When Talus/Seppo continued, Eva had to strain her ears to hear his voice.

"If only it had failed.

"I will spare the listener of this record and account the excruciating pain I went through inside the forge as my script was activated and the armor began to meld itself to and then, consume me. The pain caused me to lose all consciousness. When I awoke, I was lying outside the First Forge, my apprentice weeping over my body.

"When I opened my eyes and spoke to him, Ilmaren jumped back in fright and struck me with a hammer. Looking down at my body, I saw the reason for his fright. I was still in the armor. However, I realized there was no physical remnant of *me* inside the armor. My memory and consciousness or, as some would call it, my soul, were all that remained of the man known as Talus.

"Now that I had become immortal, I did not find it glorious. I was an abomination. I confess terror filled me — I had no way of knowing how long the imbibed rune scripts would last and expected to die at any moment."

Eva thought back to her conversation with Seppo that night in camp: *The things I remember are strange: the feel of the sun on my face, water running through my hands, grass beneath my feet, the touch of a loved one — I may be protected from age, disease, and weapons in this shell, but I have come to learn that it keeps out more than it lets in.*

"I fled Palantis that night. I attempted to take a boat off the island but it capsized and I sank to what I thought would be a watery grave. It took several minutes to realize I did not need to draw breath — was I truly alive? I sank to the bottom of the ocean and walked to the shore.

"I wandered for many years in self-imposed exile. I, Talus, who had once been counted among the mightiest in the empire, was now an outcast. It took many years to come to terms with my fate but eventually, I returned to Palantis.

"My homecoming was not as I expected. I was betrayed. Ilmaren convinced the Senate I was an abomination and they locked me away deep in the catacombs beneath the palace. I marveled at how great my fall was: from Rune Master to monster.

"Ilmaren came to me one night and, in our conversation, I saw his true self: he was a bitter, envious boy. He had continued my research and incorporated even more blood magics and dark runes into my design. Moreover, he had convinced the citizens that he could offer them a gift only the gods should ever have — immortality. The Palantines, in their pride and vanity, would have given him anything. "

Talus/Seppo stopped again and a cold chill crawled over Eva. She knew what came next but listened on, the hopes of finding some hint at how she could destroy the rune master's work.

"The corrupted First Forge gave the citizens what Ilmaren promised: in their iron armor, they were impervious to pain, sickness, and age. Thousands flocked to Palantis, drawn by the promise of life everlasting. Bound in my prison by Ilmaren's rune magic, I could do nothing to stop them. When the number of golems swelled beyond reckoning, Ilmaren completed his vile, treacherous design: he cast himself into the First Forge and emerged as the dark golem, Ogunn. All those who had gone before him were turned to mindless slaves and forced to serve his every command — the first Smelterborn.

"A hundred years of blood and war ensued. My people, the proud and mighty Palantines, were slowly destroyed by a runesmith's apprentice. By the time I escaped my prison, there were hardly any left to oppose the Smelterborn.

"And now we come to the time I record this message, using the rune box I created so long ago in my innocent experimentations. I have returned to the island of Palantis with all that remains of my people. In addition to being slaughtered by Smelterborn, they have been wracked with disease and hunted by the rebellious primitives on the mainland. The high bloodlines are all but extinct. Those few left who can fight have joined me, in a last desperate attempt to destroy Ogunn and the First Forge.

Talus/Seppo paused. For a moment, Eva thought the voice had gone for good and despaired — she still had no idea what she needed to do. When the voice returned, it spoke in a heavy, reluctant tone.

"It is my belief that a willing victim may cast themselves into the First Forge and, with this sacrifice, undo its corrupt evil power. As I am the one responsible for the complete destruction of my people, it is only fitting that the sacrifice be mine.

"I make this record in the event we fail at this task. Perhaps, one day, someone may find this account and use this knowledge to destroy the First Forge. Be warned: whoever enters the First Forge will not survive. It is my hope that my death will end the great evil I have unleashed upon the Palantines and, in some small way, make amends for my great folly. These are the last words of Talus, former Rune Master of Palantis, now a wretched abomination of his own making. Goodbye."

The light faded and the voice ended. With a shaking hand, Eva retrieved her Wonder — the Aithos stone — and threaded it back on its chain. When she placed the stone around her neck, the burden of her task pulled at her as if she was wearing a millstone.

Why had Seppo's sacrifice not completely destroyed the First Forge? It seemed he had only managed to put the golems to sleep — albeit for a very long time — until Eva's father found the Wonder stone and inadvertently brought Seppo back to life, along with Ogunn and the Smelterborn.

Eva held the stone in her palm as it turned the same shade of blue as the lantern above — the same shade of blue as Seppo's eyes. She thought back to when she'd touched the stone to Seppo's chest plate. It was almost as if a piece of Talus existed in the Wonder...

An idea formed in Eva's mind: what if Seppo hadn't been able to destroy the First Forge because he wasn't human anymore? Perhaps he had survived because a piece of his soul — the Aithos stone — hadn't been with him when he cast himself into the furnace?

The realization of what was required struck Eva like a hammer blow. But rather than being afraid, a calm settled over her. Her mind had never been more clear. She had a purpose now. She had a plan.

Chapter 27

Eva caught a glimpse of sunlight ahead and ran as fast as she could, bursting outside into the orange, fiery glow of late evening. The moon shone faint on the edge of the dying sky but promised to be at full glory come nightfall. She wasn't too late.

Hearing her approach, the gryphons shot up spraying sand everywhere. Fury, Lucia, and Carroc rushed to greet her. In his excitement, Fury almost knocked her over, keening with joy as he rubbed his beak against her shoulder. In spite of the dire circumstances, Eva laughed and ruffled her gryphon's head feathers. There had been a time in the caves when she wasn't sure if she'd ever see Fury again and felt grateful for the small mercy.

Her smile faded, however, upon seeing the concerned looks of the other gryphons.

"It's okay," she said, running her hands down Lucia and Carroc's beaks. "I've got a plan to free them. It's going to be alright."

Truth be told, Eva knew it would still take a miracle for one woman and three gryphons to free their friends and destroy the First Forge. At least they had a chance now.

By now, the sun had fallen behind the cliffs and ruins of Palantis. Time grew short. Especially Eva's.

The gryphons paced the beach restlessly, watching the full moon rising in the night sky.

Walking away from Fury and the others, Eva stopped at the edge of the short beach, watching the waves lap into shore. She'd only seen the ocean once before in Pandion. Although it's white sands and blue water far outshone the bland, bleak waters of the eastern ocean, Eva still appreciated the sight.

A warm sea breeze blew through Eva's hair, heralding the fair days of summer ahead: Days of soaring through clear blue skies with Fury, bathed in sunlight. Days with Tahl, walking through the summer markets in Gryfonesse. Days she would never see.

Eva closed her eyes, letting the sound of the waves and the feel of the wind wash over her in a few last moments of peace. When she opened them, she withdrew the Wonder from beneath her mail and cupped it in her hands. Its soft glow reassured her and warmth spread throughout her body, pushing away death's shadow.

She unbuckled the straps of her Windsworn armor and bent over to slide the mail shirt over her head. Eva felt a greater weight than just the steel rings and lacquered leather falling away. The armor, like her fears, would only slow her down.

When she returned to the gryphons, Eva wrapped her arms around Fury, burying her face in his neck feathers to hide the tears. She thought of all they'd been through since that day so long ago when she'd found Ivan hiding with a blood-red gryphon egg inside of Soot's woodshed.

"I guess we lived up to the expectations after all," Eva said, recalling the prophecies surrounding the birth of a red gryphon. She looked in Fury's fierce yellow eyes. "We've come a long way together, boy. Let's end this."

The last rays of sun winked out as Eva took to the sky on Fury with Lucia, and Carroc winging close behind. Down below, the great circle in the midst of the ruined palace courtyard was wreath in flame from hundreds of burning braziers and cauldrons. Rows and rows of dark-armored shapes surrounded the central place — Ogunn's Smelterborn witnessing their master complete his vile work.

Eva hadn't thought it possible, but the First Forge pulsed with unnatural rune fire, brighter and hotter than when they'd passed over it coming to the island. It burned like a beacon set to rival the full moon above, sending waves of dread and heat alike from its dull gray walls.

Although they were far above, Eva spotted what could only be Ogunn inside the circle, Seppo in chains next to him. Farther back, other, smaller shapes were just visible in the glow of the fires: Tahl, Ivan, Soot, Chel, and Wynn.

Now that she saw him again, and knowing all Seppo had gone through, Eva's heart went out to the Palantine-turned-golem. She couldn't imagine what it would be like to see everything you loved destroyed by something you created. Or to face years and years of blame and regret afterward. She wondered if he now viewed his days as Seppo, when he had no memory of being the rune master Talus, as simple bliss.

Eva's eyes roved over the ruins, knowing her time was short. A wall stood on the eastern side, butting up against the gathered Smelterborn, riddled with empty windows and door frames that looked like pockmarks in the stone. The First Forge sat a stone's throw away from the wall — the closest cover available.

Eva turned Fury away. She'd seen all she needed to see. The other gryphons followed in her wake and they landed back on the beach again. Eva explained everyone's role — Lucia and Carroc would provide a distraction while Fury landed Eva on the backside of the wall, where she would climb through the ruins and drop down into the courtyard when the golems were distracted. From there, she hoped to herself, there would be a clear shot to the First Forge.

The gryphons dipped their heads in understanding and Eva swung onto Fury's back. She felt her insides twist and wrench not with nervousness but with regret. She realized, as Fury spread his powerful wings and leaped into the air, that this was her last flight, the last moments she would share with her gryphon companion.

In spite of herself, Eva felt tears running down her face as Fury flew low through the sagging towers and caved in ruins of the palace. He landed on a large slab of stone jutting out from the back side of the interior courtyard wall. A window frame to their right glowed like noonday from the light shining from the First Forge.

Eva slid from Fury's back, her limbs growing heavy. She stood in front of Fury, holding his gigantic eagle's head with her hands, staring into his eyes.

"You be a good boy, okay?" she said. "Take care of them after — while I'm gone."

Fury let out a tiny chirp, reminding Eva of the long-ago days when he'd been an angry hatchling, eager to nip and scratch at her whenever he got the chance. The weight of the memories caused Eva to collapse against the red gryphon. She forced herself to pull away when Ogunn began speaking in the courtyard below, the ruins echoing his booming, ancient words.

"Good luck, boy," Eva said, squeezing Fury one last time. He shook his head and puffed out his feathers to reassure her and then launched off the stone slab with his hind paws, gliding away into the night.

"Goodbye," Eva whispered, watching him disappear into the darkness.

Eva made her way to the window opening and crouched down to watch Ogunn below. She couldn't explain why, but she felt the need to wait until the golem was at the peak of his incantations before making her move. The flames billowing from the First Forge grew as the chanting continued until a pillar of fire blasted hundreds of feet into the air. Eva thanked her good fortune — the added light from the flames would mask the approach of the gryphons.

Bound in black chains, Seppo struggled and shouted to Ogunn in what Eva guessed must be ancient Palantine. The black-armored golem ignored his former master and spread his arms higher as he chanted, the Deimos stone glowing in his hand. Eva's Wonder began to pulse and surge and she folded her arms over her chest to cover it up.

Her loved ones were on the steps below Seppo and Ogunn, chained and kneeling. Momentary relief surged through Eva. Aside from a few cuts and scrapes, they were all alive: Wynn, Ivan, Chel, Tahl, Soot.

Just seeing them gave Eva strength and she wished she could call out to them and let them know everything would be okay.

A series of gryphon screams split the air as Fury, Lucia and Carroc burst from the darkness above. Illuminated in the light of the flaming pillar, the gryphons made a fierce sight, smashing into the Smelterborn on the western side of the courtyard. Surprised by the unexpected attack, the golems toppled over, several of their counterparts falling as well due to their close quarters. Before the golems could recover, the gryphons rose and landed in the midst of the Tahl and the rest.

Ogunn's hands fell and he roared in frustration, striding toward them. Seeing her chance, Eva pulled herself over the lip of the stone window frame and extended her arms down as far as she could before dropping. She hit the stone hard but rolled on instinct, lessening the impact.

Leaping to her feet she rushed to Seppo, who looked up at her in surprise. Eva drew her sword and swung, cutting through his black chains just as Ogunn turned.

Seppo let out a roar of his own and rose, stretching his arms to snap the last of the chains binding him. He turned to Ogunn, who stood at the bottom of the steps, gigantic iron fists clenched. The Smelterborn began to advance, but the dark golem raised a hand to hold them back.

"No!" he shouted. As one, the ranks of golems froze in place, awaiting their next order.

"I knew you would come — I sensed the Aithos drawing near," Ogunn said. He raised the hand ruined by Eva's blade. "Before you die, you will watch as I feed your friends to the fires, making them my slaves for all eternity."

"I am Queen Evelyn Vakarin of Rhylance," Eva replied, her voice carrying across the courtyard. "And I have come to put an end to your abominations."

Ogunn laughed and shook his head. "Foolish mortal, do you think you can stop me? You will need more than a pretty rock and an inscribed blade for that."

"Enough!" Seppo placed himself between Eva and Ogunn,

blocking their view of one another. "Let us end this, Ilmaren."

Eva felt the blistering heat of the First Forge to her right, its pillar of orange and red rune fire stretching higher and higher into the sky as if to burn the heavens. The sweltering heat from the enchanted furnace was at the point of overwhelming the humans and Eva felt her vision spin. She judged the distance to the forge, hoping she would be able to make it to the furnace before Ogunn or the Smelterborn realized her purpose.

Thunder boomed across the clear sky as if the ancient Palantine gods pounded hammer and anvil. The island shook. A flash of green light split the air above them and Seppo moaned, sinking to his knees. Pale wisps of smoke poured from the openings of his helmet and the runes carved into his armor.

"You are too late, girl!" Ogunn proclaimed over the thunder and howling flames. "The ritual is complete: the First Forge will consume its creator and my reign will truly begin!"

Chapter 28

Seppo collapsed and Eva rushed to his side. Before them, Ogunn let out a deep booming laugh as dark flames wreathed his armor.

"Seppo, get up!" she screamed, slapping his breastplate. "Get up, I need you!"

Seppo groaned, his blue eyes flickering. In desperation, Eva reached into her shirt and yanked the Wonder from its chain. She pressed the stone to the golem's armor. Seppo's eyes shone bright once more. He attempted to rise only to have his strength give away once more.

"He is finished!" Ogunn said, his proclamation mixed with the screams of Eva's friends.

"Seppo," Eva said, leaning close to the golem's helmet so only he could hear her. "I heard your message, in the silver box. I know what to do. But I can't do it without you."

Seppo's head lolled toward hers. Eva's Wonder glowed, brighter and brighter, a perfect shade of blue. Seppo moaned again and clamped a hand over the stone of his breastplate.

"What is this trickery?" Ogunn hissed, as Seppo's fingers curled around the Wonder. "What are you doing?"

The dark golem bounded up the steps toward them. Golden light burst from the Wonder in Seppo's hand.

"Go, mistress Evelyn!"

Surging to his feet, Seppo met Ogunn in a terrible clash of iron.

Eva darted past them and heard Tahl, Soot and the rest yelling at her from across the courtyard. She shot a wild glance at them as the Smelterborn closed in, forcing the gryphons into the air to combat them. Whatever spell Ogunn had used to hold their bindings gave way when he engaged Seppo and the humans picked up the lengths of iron chain, swinging them overhead as Smelterborn closed in.

Eva glanced back at the two golems grappling with one another. Seppo struck his former apprentice like a battering ram in the side of the helmet. Ogunn reeled and Seppo pushed his advantage, hammering the black-armored golem relentlessly. Ogunn continued to retreat under the rain of blows, backing toward the First Forge.

Torn by indecision, Eva took an unsure step toward her friends. But more Smelterborn closed in, blocking her path to them as well. Her head swiveled back to Seppo and Ogunn. As the dark golem neared the First Forge, his strength recovered. Seppo swung another haymaker, but this time, Ogunn caught it in his fist and blocked Seppo's other punch with his gauntleted forearm. Closing the distance between them, Ogunn rammed Seppo in the face with the top of his helmet.

The dark fires raged across Ogunn's armor and now it was his turn to take the upper hand, raining blow and blow upon Seppo, who staggered back toward the steps where Eva stood.

Unable to reach her loved ones or the First Forge, Eva ran to Seppo's aid, drawing her sword. As she sidestepped the brawling golems, Eva swung the blade at Ogunn's knee. To her surprise, the strike rebounded in her hand and the dark flames shielding Ogunn's armor hissed.

"Your weapon is useless against me now, girl!" Ogunn said. He blocked Seppo with a forearm and swung at Eva with the other. She flew across the courtyard and struck the ground hard, head spinning.

With blurred vision, she saw Seppo continue to falter under the onslaught of Ogunn's attack. A whoosh of air blew behind her, and Eva twisted around as Fury landed beside her. The gryphon let out a worried screech and nudged her with his beak. Whether it was Ogunn's orders or Eva's Wonder that had held the Smelterborn back, they seemed to disregard it now. Stepping in unison, the golems closed in, their shields forming a wall to push everyone closer to the First Forge. Eva wrapped her hand around Fury's wing and pulled herself up, shaking her head to clear away the dizziness.

Seppo fell to the ground again as whatever strength he'd found in the Wonder faded. He looked to Eva, helpless and raised a weak arm to block Ogunn's incoming strike. Bellowing, Ogunn punched Seppo in the head once, twice, with blows that would have shattered an anvil. Pale smoke billowed out of Seppo's helmet and chest runes.

Eva looked down and spotted her sword on the ground. She bent over to retrieve it, the weapon suddenly feeling heavier than a forge hammer.

"Help him, boy!" she yelled at Fury.

Fury leaped into the air and struck Ogunn in the back with all his might as the golem stood over Seppo. The dark golem spun around, batting at the gryphon but Fury pulled away too fast.

With Ogunn temporarily distracted, Eva staggered forward as fast as her battered body would move. Ogunn turned his back to her, fending off Fury's attack and Eva swung her sword back and hurled it toward Seppo. The blade clanged off the ground and Seppo rolled over pulling it into his fist with outstretched fingers.

"Go, Evelyn!" he shouted.

Summoning the last of her strength, Eva half ran, half limped toward the forge, willing her broken body to go faster.

Twenty paces.

She glanced to her right and saw Fury spin out of the air as Ogunn's fist gripped his wing and yanked him down. The heat of the forge scorched Eva's face.

Ten paces.

Seppo staggered to his feet, clenching the rune sword. Ogunn spun away from Fury and saw Eva nearing the mouth of the Forge. The intense heat instantly dried the sweat from her body and scorched Eva's hair. She held up a hand to block the blinding light.

Five paces.

Eva's whole body screamed for respite. Three steps away, her injured leg buckled and she fell to the ground.

Ogunn roared and sprinted for her. Behind the dark golem, illuminated in the hellish glow of the forge, Eva saw Seppo leap, driving the rune sword through the back of Ogunn's helmet. The blade flared white-hot like the day it had been forged as it pierced through the front of Ogunn's helmet. The black flames on Ogunn's body quenched in an instant. Eva crawled forward and pulled herself to her feet.

She stood at the mouth of the forge now and the flames licked at her, hotter than anything she had ever imagined. She didn't how she hadn't been burned to a crisp already.

"EVA!"

She heard Tahl's screams but refused to look at him, afraid she would lose her nerve.

Closing her eyes, Eva took one last step and fell forward into the mouth of the First Forge.

Chapter
29

Tahl watched Eva give herself to the flames and screamed. Screamed like he wouldn't have thought possible until his throat burned like the fires of the First Forge itself. Eva disappeared in an instant as the flames engulfed her. He twisted in the iron embrace of the Smelterborn holding him until it felt like his arms would tear from his shoulders. It did no good.

The sky shook again, thunder booming so loud many of the half-standing walls around them crumbled and fell, crushing the Smelterborn beneath them.

A flash of white light burst from the mouth of the forge, knocking the host of golems around them to the ground. Still wrapped in the Smelterborn's arms, Tahl fell hard. His head snapped back and collided with the golem's breastplate. Everything went dark.

Sometime later, Tahl's eyes fluttered open. Groaning, he rolled over and realized he was lying next to the Smelterborn who'd been about to crush him. Dazed, Tahl stared at the golem for a moment before coming to his senses and scrambling away. The Smelterborn didn't move — the orange fires beneath its helmet extinguished.

The golem's armor started corroding away before his eyes until it was nothing more than a pile of rusted filings. Everything came rushing back.

Eva!

Fighting his pounding head, Tahl clambered to his feet and ran to the First Forge. The domed top was split in half, the runes dull. The hellish heat and flames were gone.

Eva's body lay upon a pile of ash.

Morning sunlight streamed down through the crack in the dome, illuminating her golden hair.

A wounded cry escaped his lips and Tahl fell to his knees beside his love. He eased his shaking hands beneath Eva and gently turned her over. Somehow, the flames hadn't consumed her but it made little difference. Her head lolled back, eyes closed, body limp. Aside from a smudge of ash on her face, she could have been sleeping.

But she was gone.

Sobs wracking his body, Tahl fell over Eva and clutched her as his tears fell into the ash. Gathering her in his arms, Tahl carried his love out of the ruins of the First Forge and laid her beneath the morning sun on the pale stone of the courtyard.

Moments later, a heavy hand settled on Tahl's back. He turned and found Soot, Wynn, Chel, and Ivan standing over him. Each of them stared down at Eva, tears coursing down their smoke-blackened faces.

A heartbreaking scream cut through the silence and Fury bounded forward to his rider. The red gryphon nudged Eva's cheek with his beak. When she didn't respond, he sank down on all fours on the opposite side of Tahl. Fury's head dipped to the ground and he let out a quiet chirp once, then fell silent.

"Not her!" Tahl screamed. His heart-wrenching protests echoed throughout the empty city.

The sky was a clear, bright blue — the same color as Eva's eyes, Tahl bitterly reflected. The Smelterborn continued to decay around them until all that remained were piles of corroded dust. All was as it should have been, except Eva was gone. Chel and Wynn clutched each other, shaking. Soot just stared, silent tears running down his face. A broken, grief-stricken dirge rose from Ivan as he fought his emotions to honor the Queen of Rhylance.

A mechanical groan rose behind them and the group turned. It was Seppo.

The golem crawled toward them, the lower half of his body unmoving as he stretched out and pulled himself forward with one hand, the other dragging behind, clenched. Ivan fell silent when the golem reached Eva's side.

"You did this!" Tahl screamed, his face twisted with rage and agony. "She's dead because of you!"

The glowing blue orbs inside Seppo's helmet flickered as he looked down at Eva.

"I...no..."

His garbled and broken voice fell silent. Tahl shook his head, overcome by grief. He unclenched his shaking fists and brushed away a strand of hair blown across Eva's face by the gentle breeze stirring around them.

Seppo groaned and stretched out his closed hand. Slowly, his fingers curled open to reveal the Aithos stone — Eva's Wonder. Tahl lifted the stone from Seppo's palm and the white stone gave a weak flicker. He arranged the necklace around Eva's neck, vision blurred with tears. The light of the stone blinked once more then faded away.

"Th-thank you," Seppo gasped, his voice fading. "For being... my...friendssss..."

The golem's head fell forward and his armored body fell still.

"Seppo?" Soot knelt down beside his longtime companion. He gave the golem's shoulders a gentle shake. "Come on you old rust bucket, get up."

Seppo didn't respond. All that remained of the friendly golem was an empty suit of armor. Whatever rune magic had once given him life was gone.

Tahl looked down at Eva again. In death, she looked at peace. He closed his eyes willing it all to go away, to find himself back on their ledge at the Gyr in each other's arms.

Someone coughed.

Wild hope surged through Tahl and he looked down at Eva. The white stone on her breast rose as she took a ragged gasp of air. Woman and Wonder flickered back to life.

Eva's eyes opened and she saw Tahl kneeling over her.

"Eva?" he said in a disbelieving voice. "Eva!"

Soot, Ivan, Wynn, and Chel crowded around them shouting, laughing and crying. Suddenly a huge feathered head knocked them all away and Fury let out a screech of joy, rubbing his beak against Eva's neck.

Eva groaned and Tahl helped her sit up, with the aid of several trembling hands. She looked down at her feet and saw Seppo's still body lying on the courtyard stone.

"He saved you!" Soot said, tears running down his face. "He brought you back to life!"

Soot's words cut through Eva's confused and foggy mind. "Ogunn!" she yelled, glancing around, eyes wide. "The Smelterborn!"

"They're gone, Eva," Tahl said, wiping the tears from his face and smearing it with ash and charcoal in the process. "You did it. They're all gone. The First Forge is destroyed."

Eva's heart sank as she looked at Seppo and realized that he too was no more.

"It's okay," Soot said, sniffing and wiping the back of his good hand across his nose. He heaved out a deep breath, shoulders drooping, then looked at Seppo. A small smile crossed the smith's face. "He's at peace now. And he gave you back to us."

"But…how?" Eva trailed off. "I should be dead!"

"It was the Wonder." Ivan pointed to the stone which had fallen into Eva's lap. "Whatever power Seppo imbued it with, whatever life it held brought you back."

Eva stared down at the stone, its surface swirling with a blend of gold, rose and cerulean light. She thought of her father, and his golden gryphon, Sunflash, of their courage and daring. She thought of her uncle Adelar, his love for Rhylance and its people. And she thought of Sigrid and Sven and their loyalty. Last of all, she thought of Seppo. Their sacrifices hadn't been meaningless. They hadn't died in vain.

"What now, your highness?" Tahl asked. He winked a bloodshot eye and Eva saw that familiar, cocky smirk on his face. Smiling, she reached around his neck and pulled him close.

Soot gave an awkward cough, and Wynn a gagging noise before their lips parted.

Eva looked at the others and shook her head, laughing. An old smith, an outcast plains warrior, two gryphon riders and...her. A scared, awkward smith's assistant who had somehow become a queen. Together, they'd done the impossible. They'd stopped the iron storm.

Eva stood and leaned against Fury, swaying on unsteady feet. The red gryphon gave her another reassuring nudge and Lord Vyr's pronouncement came to mind as she looked from Fury's eagle head to his lion's body.

"The eagle, the lion and the queen," she whispered. "How about that?"

With help, Eva swung onto Fury's back, Chel climbing up behind her. Mounted on Lucia and Carroc, the others waited for her to take to the sky.

She smiled. "Let's go home."

Chapter 30

"You sure about this?" Soot asked in his usual, gruff voice. "Doesn't seem fitting for some lowly smith to crown the Queen of Rhylance."

Eva laughed. "Don't you try to get out of this. You promised!"

Soot held up his metal hand, newly fitted to replace the one tarnished and battered from their journey. "What if I drop it?"

Eva rolled her eyes and stood on her tip-toes to kiss him on the cheek. "You'll be fine."

They were in Adelar's private chambers in the citadel. Eva took a deep breath and examined herself in the long mirror while Wynn fussed with her white dress. It was a thing of beauty, woven with gold and silver so that it shimmered like her Wonder whenever she moved. The white stone hung from her neck, winking and sparkling as a reminder of Seppo, the friendly golem.

Chel, her hair braided with flowers, held Eva's rune sword in her hands with its gold-chased scabbard and belt. Soot frowned at it.

"I still don't know what kind of queen wears a sword to her coronation and wedding."

"A warrior queen," Chel said with a grin as she buckled it around Eva's waist.

Wynn made her last adjustments and stepped back to admire Eva.

The young Windsworn cut a dashing figure herself in the royal blue of the gryphon riders combined with a silver cloak, marking her a member of the Queen's Wing.

The study door opened and Andor stood before them in his finest uniform, armor polished until it gleamed like a precious gem. "Ready, your highness?" he asked, grinning.

"I told you not to call me that!" Eva said. But a smile tugged at her lips and she held out her arms for Andor and Soot to escort her. Wynn and Chel took their places behind to carry Eva's train.

They walked slowly through the empty hall, Eva's heart racing as the guards came to attention. The doors opened and a wave of jubilation hit them.

All of Gryfonesse seemed to be packed into the courtyard and palace grounds. The crowd cheered and laughed as they passed, tossing flower petals to line the path of their new queen. Eva fixed a nervous smile on her face and butterflies fluttered in her stomach from the sheer number of people watching her.

Farther down the corridor, rows of visitors from Pandion and Maizoro, in addition to Scrawls and even a few Juarag, waited to pay their respects to the Queen of Rhylance. Eva nodded to the Scrawl Elders, Belka, and Arapheem as she passed by. The old Juarag raider inclined his head, a measure of how far they'd come over the previous months.

Beyond the foreigners, a line of Windsworn, both riders and gryphons, stood at attention. The summer sun glinted off their winged helms and the gryphons joined together in a wild scream when Eva reached them, sending a chill down her back.

At the front of the line, Eva saw Fury and Ivan. The red gryphon's copper-colored feathers and fur shone like burnished steel. He ruffled his head and clawed at the stone flagging in anticipation. Ivan shot Eva a reassuring grin and gestured toward the man standing beside him.

Tahl.

He looked like a hero straight out of a Scrawl's legend in his shining armor and golden cloak. When he winked at Eva her heart fluttered like the first time she'd seen him all those years before in the market.

"You're beautiful," he said when Soot and Andor stepped back and Eva took his hands.

The sounds of the crowd and Ivan's words wedding them together fell way as Eva and Tahl looked into one another's eyes. She stirred when the Scrawl stopped speaking and they turned to face him.

"Please kneel."

Eva and Tahl dropped to one knee as Soot crowned Eva and Andor did the same for Tahl. When they rose, a thunderous cheer filled the palace grounds, rising into the clear blue sky above. The applause lasted for several long moments until Ivan raised his hands for quiet. When the last shouts and claps faded, Ivan grasped Eva and Tahl's wrists and lifted their hands overhead.

"All hail Queen Evelyn Vakarin and her husband, King Tahl! Long may they reign with fair winds under peaceful skies!"

The end?

The gryphons will return.

Author's Note

Gryphons first captured my attention years ago when, as a young, impressionable kid (well under the suggested age for "Teen" video games) I was introduced to Warcraft II: Tides of Darkness by some irresponsible older cousins. Whenever I got kicked off the computer and had to *gasp* play outside, I often took on the imaginary mantle of said gryphon riders on my many childhood adventures. When it came time to start a new series, the noble gryphon riders resurfaced again and the Windsworn were born.

Writing the Gryphon Riders Trilogy has been my most rewarding and challenging project to date. My goal from the onset was to create a fresh take on "dragon rider" fantasy books with plenty of new ideas and familiar tropes mixed together. Of course, like everything fantasy I write, I threw in a splash of frontier fantasy and medieval western elements just for flavoring. Altaris, if you hadn't gathered, has many features similar to North America: the formidable Windswept Mountains much like the Rockies with the Endless Plains and the Juarag taking the place of the Great Plains and its Native American tribes. On top of that, I laid a hodgepodge of other features: Ice Age animals, a shifted equator (if you were wondering why it's warmer to the north and colder to the south in Altaris) and the shadowed remains of an Atlantean/Grecian empire.

In short, I had a blast creating this world and I hope you had just as much fun venturing into it with Eva and company. I've got many *more* plans for Altaris and I hope you'll come back and visit many more times.

If you're reading this then chances are you've stuck with me through all three books. You don't know how much that means to me. Writing isn't always some mythical, magical thing: it's often frustrating and lonely. I'm not saying that to complain — I love being an author. I say that because it's readers like **you** that make it all worthwhile. Thank you.

On that note, if you want to be even *more* awesome, one of the greatest things you could do is write a review for this book (or any of my books). Or, if reviewing isn't your thing, just recommend them to a friend! If you feel the inclination to do either of those things, you can find a complete list of all of my books on the next page.

Until next time, thank you again. Here's wishing you fair winds and clear skies.

— **DAS** (Derek Alan Siddoway)

Want More Awesome Books?

Now that you've finished the Gryphons Riders Trilogy don't miss out on a free copy *Out of Exile*, the first book in the *Teutevar Saga* series, as well as two exclusive Teutevar Saga origin stories, special perks, sneak peeks and more just by joining my newsletter, The Athelon Archives.

Click here and become an Atheling today!
If you've already joined, tell your friends!

http://derekalansiddoway.com/newsletter/

Also by the author

Gryphon Riders Trilogy

Windsworn (Gryphon Riders Book 1)

Windswept (Gryphon Riders Book 2)

Windbreak (Gryphon Riders Book 3)

Teutevar Saga

Into Exile (Teutevar Saga Book 0)

Out of Exile (Teutevar Saga Book 1)

Return to Shadow (Teutevar Saga Book 2)

Other Works

Lone Wolf Anthology: A dark and heroic fantasy collection

Swords for Hire: A Frontier Fantasy and
Medieval Western Story Anthology

Valiant (short story)

Derek Alan Siddoway

Derek Alan Siddoway is the author of Teutevar Saga, a medieval western/frontier fantasy series, and Gryphon Riders, a young adult fantasy trilogy. He was born and raised in the American West at the foot of the Uinta Mountains. An Undaunted and Everyday Author, Derek spends his free time reading, obsessively filling notebooks, adventuring outdoors and celebrating small victories. He's also a sucker for Star Wars and football, namely the University of Utah and Minnesota Vikings.

For more shenanigans, find Derek online in the following places:

@D_Sidd (Twitter)
Teutevar Saga (Facebook)
derekalansiddoway.com

Made in the USA
Monee, IL
18 June 2022

98217566R00125